SACRIFICES

SACRIFICES

DRAGON APPROVED™ BOOK SEVEN

RAMY VANCE

MICHAEL ANDERLE

DISRUPTIVE IMAGINATION

THE SACRIFICES TEAM

Thanks to the JIT Readers

John Ashmore
Kathleen Fettig
Kelly O'Donnell
Diane L. Smith
Larry Omans
Deb Mader

If we've missed anyone, please let us know!

Editor
The Skyhunter Editing Team

LMBPN Publishing
PMB 196, 2540 South Maryland Pkwy
Las Vegas, NV 89109

First US Edition, March 2020
Version 1.01, October 2020
eBook ISBN: 978-1-64202-823-2
Print ISBN: 978-1-64202-824-9

DEDICATION

To the GGW Team... here's to one hell of a year!

—Ramy

*To Family, Friends and
Those Who Love
to Read.
May We All Enjoy Grace
to Live the Life We Are
Called.*

— Michael

CHAPTER ONE

In the green valleys of Middang3ard, the sky grew dark and oppressive. There was a storm coming, a much larger one than what played out in the sky. The flashing crimson lightning was only a foretaste of what was to come.

All throughout the land, folks eyed the sky with growing mistrust. There hadn't been blood clouds like this for a long time, long enough that many people had forgotten what they foretold. Yet the fear was there.

Parents hid their children inside, tucking them in early before the true night descended. They hoped blankets and candles would ward off any danger, hoped dreams would protect the young innocents.

Not all children were home; there were some who had left their homes. They had come to Middang3ard to fight in the war to end all wars. Those children stood in a valley underneath the large mass of black clouds in the gray sky, staring up at the blood-red streaks of lightning as their friend plummeted toward the earth.

Alex was watching the sky, watching the horror unfolding above her. Brath had been unanchored from Furi, who was falling, madly flapping his wings, trying to fly. Whatever had hit them must have been incredibly strong. Alex couldn't imagine anything that could hurt Furi that much.

The world seemed to be in slow motion. Even though Alex knew Brath was falling and there was something she needed to do about it, there didn't seem to be a rush. Brath fell so slowly.

Gill's scream punctured the time distortion, and Alex felt everything return to speed. Her eyes focused without her realizing it, and she could see Brath's eyes, wide with fear, as he turned, still falling.

Alex turned to Jollies and shouted, "Help him!"

Jollies pulled up on Amber and flew toward Brath. Gill was already on Timber, pulling the dragon into the air. They both raced toward Brath.

Above Brath floated a meteor. The meteor should have fallen hours ago, but it was not truly a rock. It hung in the air like a blade waiting to drop. Alex still wasn't sure what the object was. First, a wizard had emerged from it. Now giant bees, vrosks, and bats were flying out through a hole in the side.

These creatures headed for Brath, swarming in a mass of black wings flapping mindlessly as if they were denizens of hell released upon the world of the living.

Gill broke away from Jollies, heading straight for the closest beasts, those who looked as if they were getting close enough to strike Brath. The drow slipped under them, his dragon Timber blasting up a concussive force from his mouth that pushed the black-winged bats back.

Timber maneuvered under Brath so the gnome fell onto his back. Gill checked to see if the gnome was okay.

Brath was still breathing, but his face was badly burned, and he was now unconscious. Gill turned Timber around, ignoring the creatures from the meteor as he hit his comm. "Brath is hurt," Gill explained. "We're coming down."

Jollies and Amber were flying around Furi. They were spraying a healing salve on the dragon, working as fast as they could. They hoped the salve would wake Furi before he crashed into the ground.

That was their only option. Furi was far too large to try to support out of the sky. If the salve didn't pop the dragon's eyes open, nothing could save him.

Furi continued to fall as Jollies and Amber flew around him, still deploying the bright green healing mist. Suddenly, Furi's eyes popped open and he flapped his wings, creating a gust of wind that almost knocked Jollies off Amber.

The pixie and her dragon flew away from Furi as he regained his balance, looking around for his rider. When Furi saw Brath lying on Timber's back, Furi raced toward him as Timber landed next to the rest of the dragons and mech riders.

Alex climbed onto Timber and helped Gill lower Brath off the dragon. They placed Brath gently on a mat on the ground.

Roy walked up silently behind the remainder of Team Boundless, as did Toppinir, the elf's and the human's eyes locked on what was going on above them all. The sky grew darker still as the wings of the creatures unleashed from the meteor blocked out the light of the sun.

Roy shook his head and said, "The dark clouds would have been appreciated more than this. I see that not listening to orders runs through your entire team."

Alex stared daggers at Roy as she got to her feet and got in his face. "Do you have anything else you want to add?" she said, barely able to keep from punching him in the face.

Toppinir put himself between them. "Hey, this isn't the time," he said. "They have a man down, Roy. Lock it down."

Roy bowed, his face sincerely contrite, and said, "I am sorry."

Alex didn't want to let it go, but the sky was full of monsters, and Brath was hurt very badly. "Is there anything we can do for him?" Alex asked as she knelt next to Brath.

Roy paced, scratching the stubble on his face. "Our medic died in the first wave."

"Don't you have wizards or someone with healing magic or something?"

"Not in the mech or dragonriders. We're strictly an artillery squad. Most of the mech riders are human, and the dragonriders aren't wizards. We riders ain't known for our magic."

Toppinir was staring at the sky, his eyes nearly as dark as the clouds. "I can help him," he said softly. "My ties to magic are stronger than most here. Healing a few burns shouldn't be a problem."

With grace and solemnity, Toppinir knelt beside Brath and ran his palm over the gnome's face while murmuring softly under his breath. The air around Brath changed—grew cold and then warm. The burns on Brath's body faded like carvings on stone, weathered by wind over the years.

Brath sat up, his eyes opening sleepily as he scratched his face where the burns had been. "What the hell happened?" he asked.

Alex punched Brath in the shoulder. "You flew off like an idiot without thinking of what could happen!" she shouted, pointing at the horde of monsters in the sky. "You could have gotten yourself killed."

Brath laughed bitterly as he got to his feet. "Isn't this a suicide mission?" he asked. "Since when are we worrying if we're going to die?"

Alex didn't have an answer for Brath's snide comment. He did have a point. Arguing over who died on a suicide mission was like arguing over who was going to get the first bowl of hot soup; it didn't matter what order you were in, there was enough to go around, and it was going to get cold soon enough.

Roy and Toppinir were both transfixed by what was going on above. In a morbid way, it was beautiful. Alex had hardly seen the sky in her brief life, but she could never have imagined one looking like this.

The sky reminded her of death. She had never visualized what death looked like, but now she knew it was like this sky. Not the good kind of death, falling asleep in old age and never waking up. This death would be violent and heart-wrenching.

The rest of Alex's team came over and watched the sky with Alex, Roy, and Toppinir while the dragons gathered in the background, examining Furi's superficial wounds. All of the mech riders and dragonriders were fascinated with what was going on above. They knew it would have to be dealt with.

A creeping dread started in the back of Alex's mind, and the hairs on her neck bristled. *How are we going to kill all of them?* she wondered. It finally dawned on her that there had been no way to save Toppinir and Roy. The two hadn't been in any immediate danger, they were just up against unbeatable odds.

Roy let out a heavy sigh as he walked over to his mech and climbed in. "Okay, boys and girls, who's ready for round two?" he asked.

Alex couldn't believe what she was hearing. The man didn't sound like he had a problem with the odds they were facing. "Wait, are you serious?" she exclaimed. "Are you really thinking about going up there? Didn't you see what just happened to Brath?"

Roy lit a cigar. "No offense, but me and my squad aren't

nearly as green as you and your friends," he wheezed. "We're not going to go down in a couple of minutes. Maybe a couple of hours, a dozen if we get lucky. We'll put a dent in them no matter what."

There was a determined flavor to Roy's words. Alex had never heard anything like it. Even though she had said earlier she was ready to die, listening to Roy showed her she had been mistaken.

Alex would have fought tooth and nail to stay alive. She would have schemed and plotted and struggled to the bitter end to hold on to her life. Roy didn't have to say he was willing to give his life for the cause. It was evident in his voice, in his face. The man was all in.

Toppinir would be the voice of reason. He had to be. That must be why he and Roy always teamed up. Roy was the crazy son-of-a-gun, and Toppinir was the cool, calm, collected strategist. The elf must have a plan up his sleeve.

Much to Alex's dismay, Toppinir went to his dragon and leaped aboard, taking his seat on a saddle–the oldest tech Alex had seen since she'd gotten to Middang3ard. "More than a few hours," Toppinir said. "I'd say at least twelve unless there are more of those creatures inside of the meteor."

Alex rushed to Roy and Toppinir, waving her hands like they were capable of grounding the mech and the dragon. "Wait, aren't you even a little curious to know what that thing *is*?" she shouted. "It's obviously not a meteor. Meteors aren't full of monsters."

Roy ashed his cigar and leaned over the side of his mech. "Don't matter, since you kindly pointed out what it's doing," he said calmly. "It's dumping hundreds of vicious creatures into Middang3ard to destroy everything this realm knows. Can't see how figuring what it is will stop it from doing that."

Alex turned to Toppinir, hoping to get something other

than insanity from the elf. "Are you serious? You don't even know what that thing is," she argued. "What if we destroyed it? You saw how all those bats dropped once we killed Holmorth."

Toppinir ran his fingers through his wispy goatee. "True," he admitted. "Even then, it took an extreme amount of artillery to shave off a little piece of the meteor in question. It's unlikely we will be able to destroy it."

Roy groaned loudly. "Don't matter. There's an army of the Dark One's vermin up there, and as far as I can tell, it makes a pretty effective wall between us and whatever plan you're trying to cook up."

This was where Alex was going to put her foot down. She had more than a half-baked plan. "Okay," she said. "What's the difference between our dragons and mechs and everything up there?"

Roy chewed on his cigar as he leaned out of his mech. "All right, I'll bite," he grumbled. "What's the difference?"

Alex flashed her mischievous grin. "What's up there doesn't have four legs," she started. "Which means they expect the fight to be in the air. And only in the air."

A sparkle danced behind Roy's eyes as he caught onto what Alex was saying. "Hm. I guess there's more to you than crazy ideas. You got crazy ideas offering a little bit of hope. All right. If we're all gonna die anyway, what's the harm in trying something new?"

CHAPTER TWO

R oy, Toppinir, and Alex discussed the plan. Somehow, they were going to funnel the flying creatures to the ground. At first, it seemed like a straightforward idea. A problem eventually arose, though.

As the three were planning, Jollies casually pointed to the sky. "There's more of them than before."

When Alex looked up, she was shocked to see that Jollies was understating the case. The number of monsters had nearly doubled in the ten minutes Alex had been speaking to the two veterans. If this kept up, there would be too many of the Dark One's forces to fight in any way.

Brath sauntered over to the discussion, his face smugger than usual. "You guys are spending way too much time talking this through," he snapped. "We need to get in there and do some damage."

Toppinir chuckled under his breath before saying, "We all saw how that worked out for you. I think it would be best if we don't make the same mistake as you did."

Roy tried to hide his snickers but was unable to. Brath blushed, but he didn't back down from his point. He threw himself into the argument, defending his opinion with vigor.

At this point, Alex knew talking sensibly wasn't going to happen. The moment Brath joined a strategy session, it devolved to irritated sighing and the occasional brief but intense shouting match.

Alex went for a walk, staring at the sky. She made her way to Chine, who was sitting away from the other dragons, blasting his claws with thin streams of fire. *'Sup, Chine?*

Chine lost interest in grooming himself and peered at Alex with his large, unfathomable eyes. *Something on your mind, Dustling? You seem perturbed.*

Alex gestured upward as she sat down across from Chine. *You ever see anything like this before?*

Chine nodded as he followed Alex's gaze. *I have seen these creatures before, but I have never seen them like this. From my understanding, shooting stars rarely hold monsters. When they do, those monsters are ancient, eldritch. Not such base creatures as vrosks.*

What do you mean about shooting stars holding eldritch monsters?

Chine blew out a flame that briefly illuminated Alex's face. Her eyes were dilated, almost reptilian, nearly the same as her dragon's. *Many of the eldritch Old Ones were conceived in a place between realms.*

They were not born of flesh and blood, as many of us are. It is difficult to understand how they were conceived, but many of them were incubated in meteors and asteroids. When those rocks hit the realms, the Old Ones were born.

The meteor above was still stationary. The green aura around it spiked and withdrew as if it were a living thing. *Do you think there might be something like that in there?* Alex wondered.

Chine had grown bored looking at the sky and returned

to grooming himself. *Perhaps. But whatever is incubating inside is not an Old One. It is something new. Perhaps something worse.*

Good talk, Chine. You always know just what to say to encourage me.

How is that encouraging, Dustling?

Sarcasm, my dude. Sarcasm.

Alex sat there for some time, thinking about what the dragon had said as she watched the sky. Holmorth had been in the meteor, but he had only been on the outer crust. It was almost as if he were a guard, protecting something more important within the meteor. *What do you think we should do?* Alex asked.

Chine's scales ruffled as he stood and shook his wings. *Roy and Toppinir are not like you and the rest of Boundless. They are soldiers, and they have been soldiers for some time. They have orders and they follow them. You, on the other hand..."*

Yeah, I know, I don't listen to orders.

You say that as if it were a fault. Thinking for yourself is an admirable quality, one that dragons respect greatly. It is a quality that will never fail you. Why should now be any different?

Alex crossed her arms as she tossed herself to the grass with a loud huff. *All that it's done so far is get my friends and me in trouble. What's it going to get me this time?*

The dragon leaned over Alex, looking her in the eyes. *Perhaps victory. Or are you so weak-willed that a simple disagreement will sway you?*

Alex rolled over and sat up as she pointed at Chine. *You know what? I'm not a huge fan of this attitude. So, no. I'm not going to let it stop me. Now excuse me. I have a point to go make to Roy and Toppinir.*

Alex marched up to Toppinir and Roy, coughed as loud as she could, folded her arms, and waited for them to turn. "There's something in the meteor," she said. "Don't know what it is, but I know Holmorth was only the tip of the iceberg."

Toppinir raised his eyebrows. "It isn't an iceberg. It's a meteor," he corrected.

Roy rubbed his forehead as he sighed. "It's a human idiom," Roy explained. "You can only see the tip of an iceberg. There's a whole mess of ice underneath. What's beneath the surface usually does the damage."

"An apt analogy, then. But I believe the rest of the iceberg has vomited out into the sky already."

Alex shook her head in disagreement and said, "No, that's the thing, I don't think it has. Those monsters, all that—it's just a smokescreen for what's inside. Like, I don't know, a defense mechanism or something."

Toppinir looked interested in Alex's reasoning. "Why do you think that?"

"Why would the most powerful thing be located on the outside of the meteor, close to the surface? And as soon as we damage the rest of the meteor, more monsters come flooding out? It's to protect something. Like when you get too close to an anthill, piles of ants come out to protect the queen. There's something else in there."

Roy and Toppinir exchanged glances as they thought through what Alex had said. "All right," Roy finally said. "What do you propose?"

Alex pointed up at the monsters passively flying in the sky. "See how they haven't even attacked us yet?" she asked. "They're waiting for us to go up there. Like I said before, I say we drive them down, wipe them out, and try to crack the meteor open."

The plan wasn't any different from what had been offered before. The big difference was, it caught Toppinir's and Roy's interest this time. Throwing your life away was one thing, but the mystery of what was in the meteor made the prospect more exciting.

Toppinir, still being the voice of reason, said, "And how do you propose we do this?"

Alex held her hand out in front of her. "This is the wall of monsters," she explained. "They're all grouped together. I say we swing around from the far side and come down on top of them. That'll force them down. Sure, there'll be stragglers, but we'll catch most of them. Then we clean up the rest."

Roy pushed Toppinir away and said, "Give us a minute to talk this out."

Alex politely watched as Toppinir and Roy walked away, talking between themselves. They stood a little way off and discussed the mission prospects as the rest of Boundless came up to Alex. "What are they talking about?" Jim asked.

"My plan to figure out what's inside the meteor," Alex answered.

"Didn't we already find out what was in there? Holmorth, right?"

"No, that was just the beginning. I think whatever is in there will put Holmorth to shame."

Jollies gasped, and her hue shimmered to a deep blue. "Really? Worse than him?" she asked. "He was so strong and disgusting."

Alex noticed Roy and Toppinir walking back as she shrugged off Jollies' concern. "Yeah, Holmorth was pretty bad," Alex agreed, "but we took care of him easy enough. No casualties. And he and his drones or whatever the hell they were are dead. I think we can take it."

Toppinir and Roy joined the group, and the elf stepped forward. "We think your plan might be viable," he said. "I suggest you check on your dragons and prepare to—"

Alex cut him off. "Our dragons are already prepped. When will you be ready?"

Toppinir was caught off-guard by Alex's readiness. "Uh, give us half an hour or so. Then we'll be ready for the battle."

"Good. Hurry up. The longer we wait, the more of those monsters we'll have to deal with."

As Jollies had said, the cloud of creatures and monsters floating around the meteor had doubled. It truly looked as if the monsters had the potential to block out the sun.

The only speck of hope left was that the monsters hadn't descended and attacked. They continued to float, unaware of, or perhaps unconcerned with, the dragonriders beneath them.

Alex thought the monsters might operate like some kind of security system. If you passed a certain point, the alarm went off, and the vrosks and bats would attack. As long as they didn't pass that point, the dragonriders would be okay. The problem was figuring out what that point was.

Realistically, it couldn't be just any spot in the sky; it had to be near the meteor. That meant, in theory, there was a lot of working space for the dragonriders. It was inevitable they were going to cross the line in the sky and send the beasts into a frenzy. They just had to make sure they were in the proper position before that happened.

Roy was rallying his troops with a speech, as was Toppinir. Team Boundless watched from the sidelines. Alex didn't see the point in trying to whip her squad into a frenzy. Each of them looked ready to do what must be done.

There wasn't any doubt on their faces. Team Boundless' will was as strong as Alex's.

Also, Alex wasn't sure if she and Boundless were invited on the mission. She thought it better not to make a scene either way. *It's easier to ask for forgiveness than permission*, she thought.

Chine's voice chimed in Alex's head. *Both also stop being a problem in the face of defeat or victory. The dead can make no apologies, and victors have no need of them."*

Alex reached down and rubbed the dragon's back scales. *That's exactly what I needed to cheer me up in the most morbid way as possible.* She laughed.

I thought that would be motivating.

Roy and Toppinir pointed to the meteor in the sky, Roy shouting, "All right, mech riders, this is what we came here for. That hunk of rock is the most dangerous thing to come to Middang3ard since we did. Let's remind the Dark One why we're the stuff of his nightmares!"

Alex suddenly realized Jim wasn't with the other mech riders. "Hey, shouldn't you be with your squad?" Alex asked Jim.

Jim popped open his cockpit and leaned out. "Eh, they're not going to miss me," he said nonchalantly. "Besides, Myrddin put me with you guys. I'm Team Boundless today, whether Roy likes it or not. It's my preference anyway."

Toppinir and his dragonriders were also preparing to take off. The two veterans met each other's eyes, gave the signal (a nod more usually reserved for running into someone you didn't like at the supermarket), and took off, their riders following.

Alex didn't wait for an invitation from the veteran dragonriders. She gave the signal to Team Boundless, pointing to the meteor and the battle awaiting them. "All right, Boundless," Alex shouted, "We're going in hard from the right. Flank them from the top, then bring down hell on their heads!"

CHAPTER THREE

The dragonriders moved into position. They wasted no time, hardly making a sound as they swooped into the space between the meteor and the swarm of hellish winged creatures. Roy and Toppinir took the front line. Alex held back, watching and waiting to see what happened.

Toppinir looked over his shoulder and waved Alex over, shouting something she couldn't hear. She motioned to her comm and tapped it, and the elf's voice came through. "You don't think you're getting out of this, do you?"

As Alex urged Chine forward, she said, "I didn't know I was invited to the adult table for the party."

"Yup. It's your plan."

That was all the time they spent talking because as soon as Alex got beside Toppinir, Roy dove forward, firing missiles at the walls of creatures. His missiles weren't as strong as a dragon's breath, but it was enough to take care of a few vrosks.

Toppinir was next, his dragon shooting blue fire from its gullet in quick, controlled bursts. It wasn't enough to kill anything, but it did damage. As Toppinir fired, he pushed his dragon forward, forcing the creatures to the ground.

Alex followed Toppinir's example. Chine shot small blasts of ether fire, enough to graze the fur of the bats but not enough to set it aflame. Alex, Roy, and Toppinir headed up the attack, and the rest of the dragonriders came up on the side.

Those dragonriders took care of containing the overflow. As the three in the front forced the monsters down, a few creatures tried to flee from the scene, bolting to the right or left. The dragonriders on containment flew to the sides, blasting the monsters trying to escape and corralling them into a massive spire heading toward the ground.

Once Alex was certain the monsters were going to continue moving, she looked back at the meteor. The green aura floating over it had taken on a crystalline look, almost as if the energy had solidified into stone.

There was something else in the meteor. Alex could feel it deep in her mind as if whatever was in the meteor was reaching out to her and calling her, trying to speak. It took all of Alex's will, but she turned away from the meteor. Whatever was in there was dangerous.

The creatures continued to be forced down to the ground. Their screeches filled the air, cut off only by the combustion of the dragon fire singing skin and fur. The whooping of the dragonriders was almost barbaric.

At the rate they were going, the creatures were going to be on the ground in no time, and then the real battle would start. Alex figured it would be more like cleanup. Most of the monsters only had two legs. They wouldn't be ready for a ground fight. "We got this!" Alex shouted.

Above the dragonriders, there was a very loud click. It was an ominous sound. A switch the size of a skyscraper must have been flipped.

Alex looked up, staring at the hole Holmorth had come from in the meteor. It was glowing bright green. "Oh, crap, this is not good," Alex muttered before hitting her comm and shouting, "Hey, guys! Up above!"

The dragonriders all looked at the meteor, where energy was being pulled and charging with a twinkling of green light as if the riders were seeing a dying star.

Without warning, a blast of green energy shot from the hole in the meteor. The energy blast tore through the right side of the dragonriders' right flank, instantly killing two riders. The remaining riders on the right pulled away.

With the break in the formation, the creatures poured through the hole, flying upward to attack the three riders trying to force the winged beasts groundward.

When Toppinir saw what was happening, he turned to Alex and commanded, "Bring one of your guys up here. I'm going to handle them until the right side can get back together."

The clicking from above was followed by a whirring as if a great vortex were opening. Alex couldn't help but look in the direction of the meteor as it prepared to fire again. "Are you with me?" Toppinir shouted, bringing Alex's focus back to him.

Alex nodded and Toppinir took off toward the right of the formation, blasting the escaped monsters with his dragon's icy breath. The rest of the riders on the right side joined him. Alex hit her comm and said, "Jim, I need you on my left. Now!"

Jim's voice crackled over the comm, letting Alex know he was coming, as he swung over from the left flank of the formation, taking Toppinir's spot between Roy and Alex. He instantly started firing his flamethrower. The flames weren't as hot as a dragon's, but they got the job done.

The meteor was powering up for another shot. Alex knew

that in their current position, they were defenseless targets. There wasn't anything that could be done; it was a race against time. Could they get to the ground before the meteor tore them all apart?

Alex looked up at the meteor, focusing as hard as she could. All she needed was a clue. Luckily, her eyes were good enough to give her one.

In the middle of the green energy hole, Alex could see the faintest glint of white light. The light was moving back and forth. She assumed it was the aiming mechanism. From where she was, it looked like the meteor was going to fire on the left side, so they could switch it up and break both formations.

Alex patched to Roy. "The meteor is going to fire again, but this time it's going for the left side."

"Gotcha," Roy replied. "Left side, when you hear the thing fire, scatter. Once the beam passes, reform and take out any leftover vermin, got it?"

A chorus of "Hell, yeah" filled the comm system.

The confident response was quickly cut off by the sound of the meteor's energy beam firing again. The air grew hot and acidic with energy as another green beam rocketed toward the riders. They were barely able to swerve out of its path of destruction, narrowly missing being obliterated.

Luckily, there were no casualties this time, and since the riders had enough of a heads up, only a few creatures escaped from the tight net the riders had cast.

Alex continued to push on with Roy and Jim. Gill's voice cut into her comm. "Hey," he said. "You know that click we keep hearing? That's the meteor gearing up to fire. We have thirty or so seconds from the click until it fires. It also seems like the meteor needs to recharge for up to five minutes before each shot."

Alex was constantly impressed by Gill. Even when she

didn't know what he was doing, the drow was always thinking, working out how to get around a problem. "All right, let Roy and Toppinir know too. Maybe they can think of something."

There was a half-formed plan hatching in Alex's mind, and it had nothing to do with what Gill had just told her. That was someone else's problem. She had one right in front of her, and the solution was becoming more obvious.

Hey, Chine, how big can you make the gravity warper?

Roughly the size of the meteor above us. Give or take a few meters.

Perfect. On my call, I want you to kick it into gear, but I want the gravity field over all of these creeps. Triple it toward the ground. All right?

Understood.

Alex patched into Toppinir, Roy, and Jim. "Hey, guys, the longer we do this, the more likely it is we're going to get fried."

Roy laughed bitterly and replied, "I'm pretty sure that's the definition of a suicide mission."

"Well, I have a way to speed it up. When I say go, we push down hard, all right?"

"If it gets me out from under the giant green death ray, I'm more than happy to do it."

Alex leaned forward and shouted, "Now!" as she plunged. Chine activated his gravity field, and there was a noticeable tug downwards. Alex watched as a nearly invisible aura spread over the dragonriders and the monsters they were herding.

Then gravity really kicked in. Alex was yanked to the ground. Chine shot off small bursts of ether fire to encourage the monsters to move faster. In a few seconds, the entire seething mess of riders and monsters was rocketing down at the speed of a falling elevator.

Roy popped out of his cockpit for a second to get a better look at what was happening. "Yippee-ki-yay!" he shouted before ducking back into his mech.

The dragonriders didn't have much control at this point, but it didn't matter. The gravity well was driving everything groundward anyway. The only problem was how they were going to stick the landing. *Chine, deactivate the gravity well a few feet from the ground, all right?* Alex suggested.

Chine already knew what Alex was thinking. *Will that be enough time?*

Let's hope it is.

Alex patched into the rest of the dragonriders. "All right, guys, the gravity is going to disengage in a couple of seconds. We gotta pull up after that. Otherwise, we're going to crash into the ground, all right?"

There was a murmur of agreement as the dragonriders prepared for the last-minute change to the trajectory.

The ground was rushing up fast. Alex could hardly see it through all the beating wings beneath her, but when she caught a glimpse, she knew it was going to be a hard maneuver, even by her standards. Hopefully, it wouldn't be too much for the rest of the riders.

From above came the familiar dread-inducing click. Alex's heart sank. She assumed the same was happening for the rest of the riders. Forty-five seconds, tops. That was all they were going to have to pull this off.

Alex counted to herself as she felt the gravity start to loosen up. Chine was slowly tapering it off, giving the rest of the riders more freedom to determine how they were going to pull up.

Then the gravity cut off. Alex had lost count of how long had passed since the meteor's last click, but it didn't matter. The important thing right now was making sure she didn't go headfirst into the ground. Alex pulled up with everything she had and banked left. The rest of the riders did the same.

As the dragonriders tried to avoid the ground and move in another direction, the meteor fired, a hellblast of green energy penetrating the ground. The riders scattered like chaff in the wind, many of them being tossed around by the vacuum created by the energy beam.

The monsters weren't as lucky as the riders. Still caught in the throes of the gravity well and without competent riders, they were all but defenseless. The green energy beam cut through the monsters, turning their bodies to flames and ashes.

Alex was overjoyed as she looked over her shoulders. The green energy beam faded. "Talk about a lucky break!" she shouted.

Roy cackled over the comm. "All right, riders, let's mop this mess up!"

The dragonriders descended on the remaining monsters, Toppinir leading the charge. He started in the same fashion the riders had used to corral the monsters initially, forcing the remaining creatures out of the vantage point of the energy beam.

It was time for Alex to finish what she had started. She and Chine swooped through the vrosks and bats, which were tripping over each other, flapping their wings senselessly, trying to take to the sky again.

Chine let loose a tumult of ether fire as he flew over the creatures. The rest of the riders were doing the same—flying overhead and unleashing attack after attack on the defenseless monsters.

The mech riders had set themselves the task of containing anything trying to escape. They formed a large circle around the monsters, slowly closing it as they fired missiles at the monsters, who lashed out with their fangs and tails.

The attacks meant nothing to the mech riders. What the mechs lacked in speed and maneuverability, they made up for in defenses. They continued to push the circle tighter, undeterred by attacks, fighting their way toward each other as the numbers of the monsters dwindled.

Toppinir and his dragon rose into the air, silhouetted in the glow of the meteor above, before rocketing into the middle of the circle. The dragon hit the ground, sending a concussive force through the air along with a wall of flame, incinerating the remaining monsters.

When the smoke and flames cleared, there were only ash and bone. The day was won.

CHAPTER FOUR

The battle was over. The creatures that hadn't been obliterated by the meteor's green beam had been killed by the dragonriders. There were a few of those riders walking amongst the corpses, finishing off whatever had survived.

The rest of the dragonriders had removed themselves from the battlefield, making sure they were a good distance from the meteor's range. Many of them gazed up at the object, their hearts still racing from the battle, fearful of the meteor's power.

Despite having been in the atmosphere for some time, the meteor hadn't moved any closer. It hung in the same place it had since originally entering the atmosphere. This was cause for concern and had prompted a heated discussion amongst the riders.

Team Boundless had instantly gone to service their dragons, Alex trying to drive home the point that the comfort and safety of their dragons were the priorities outside of battle. She reminded her squad that this would put them in the position to fight again as quickly as possible.

No one from Boundless had a problem with that logic, and they broke off from the main group of riders, who were busy celebrating their victory, their dragons patiently waiting to be drained of draconian fluid.

Alex was elbow deep in Chine's spine, both of them wincing and trying to ignore their pain when Roy approached from the other dragonriders' camp. "You guys like to keep to yourselves?" Roy called to her.

The dragonrider ignored Roy at first, preferring to pay attention to the task at hand. Once Chine's fluid had been drained, it started to absorb into her body. She sat down, gritting her teeth through the pain, waiting for it to pass.

Pain, like all things, does pass. Once Alex was finished absorbing the fluid, she playfully slapped the back of her dragon's head and leaped off, sending her thoughts. *All right, gotta go see how much trouble I'm in this time.*

Chine didn't show any physical signs of having heard Alex, but she could feel the dragon chuckling inside her head. *Your strategy won the battle. Today might not be the day to ask for forgiveness.*

Roy was waiting for Alex, admiring Chine from afar as she lazily walked up. "Keep to ourselves?" Alex repeated. "Not really. We'd love to be hanging out with the big kids, but I have the sneaking suspicion we aren't wanted."

It was Roy's turn to act awkward. The man reminded Alex of a child trying to muster up the courage for an apology. Finally, Roy spoke. "Can't see why they wouldn't want you," he nearly whispered. "Good plan, by the way. Worked like a charm. Got a good head on you. Glad to see it still attached too."

"I'm planning to keep it that way. Besides, these suicide missions are starting to look more survivable. I'll probably need a head if I'm going to be doing any more."

"You were right about there being something else in the

meteor as well. I give credit where it is deserved. There must be something operating that beam."

Alex couldn't stop herself from looking up at the meteor. The hunk of rock had become something else in her eyes over the last few hours. She could see why Myrddin had been so obsessed with stopping this thing.

Regardless of what was inside the meteor, its energy beam weapon was cause enough to try to blow the damn thing up. That beam could easily take out a city. "It could all be automated," Alex suggested to Roy. "The same way the drones and those monsters were."

Roy scratched his chin as he pondered Alex's words. "True," he agreed. "Either way, a defense system implies something to defend. By the way, we're getting a squad of reinforcements and supplies. Your pal Manny is going to be there. Care to join?"

"Join what?"

"Our little war room on the ship."

"Sure. I don't have anything better to do."

Roy laughed as he headed back to the main squad. "Glad to see you have a sense of humor. We don't have enough riders with that asset. You'd think constantly risking your life would help you see the ludicrousness of life, or at least give you something to laugh at. Not these guys. Wouldn't know a joke if it walked up and punched them in the face."

"Maybe you just aren't very funny."

Roy stopped in his tracks. His face was grave as he turned to face Alex. He looked as if he had just been slapped. "Me, not funny?" he asked. "Now that's a good joke."

The two of them joined up with Toppinir, who was watching his team finally get to their dragon maintenance. Toppinir politely bowed in Alex's direction and repeated many of the accolades Roy had just stated. "The ship should be here in twenty minutes or so," he informed Alex.

The dragonriders in Toppinir's squad were talking and joking with each other. The mood in the air was almost cheery, despite the giant rock of death floating ominously overhead. "Hey, do you guys think you could call me when the ship gets here?" Alex asked. "I'd like to check in with my team."

Toppinir agreed to the request, and Roy shrugged it off as something he didn't care about. Alex headed back over the hill to Team Boundless.

The squad had finished their maintenance and was huddled around a small fire. The dragons had circled their riders. The fire was a good idea. Despite it being late afternoon, the air in the valley was cold. No doubt, it was caused by the meteor.

No one had mentioned it, but Alex felt as if the meteor was distorting the world around her. The air felt different in her lungs. The valley was far too quiet, as if it were devoid of life. It was too bright for there to be so many black clouds in the sky.

Alex sat down next to Jim, who was pulling up grass and blowing it off his palm. "Nice of you to join us," Jim chided.

Gill watched Alex and Jim from behind the flames of the team's fire. Alex could feel his eyes on her, and when she looked up, Gill didn't bother looking away. Discerning what was behind his eyes was difficult. They did not look angry or hurt, merely watchful. After a bit, Gill turned and began speaking with Jollies.

Jim picked up on the silence and cleared his throat. "Just a joke," he said. "I didn't really think you were abandoning us or anything."

Alex was brought back from her thoughts. "Huh," she murmured. "Oh, yeah, I didn't think you guys thought that or anything. Figured you were happy you weren't the ones being chewed out."

From over the fire came Brath's laugh. "Yeah, I'm not going to lie, I'm glad I missed that one. Assume you're going to be the one to lecture me, am I right?"

Alex shook her head as she leaned back against Chine's arm. "Nope. Not my place. We're a team, and we're supposed to work together. We make mistakes, and we learn together. I'll leave it at that, all right?"

"Sounds good to me."

Jollies flitted over the fire and took a seat on Alex's shoulder. "So, what's happening next?" she asked. "That meteor is still in the sky. That's why we're here, right?"

Alex glanced at the meteor before returning her gaze to the fire. She was just as likely to find answers in the dancing flames as the green aura above. "We came here to help Roy and Toppinir," she finally assented. "If their mission is the rock, then our mission is the rock."

"What are they planning on doing?"

"Reinforcements are coming, Manny along with them. I'm guessing they have orders from higher up he's delivering. I'm going to be meeting with them too. Until then, I guess we just sit tight."

Gill stood and walked over to Alex, taking a seat in front of her and Jim. Alex wished the drow wouldn't always be so direct. It was disconcerting. And confusing. Brath had said Gill liked her, but Gill didn't show his affection in any way she expected him to.

The coolness Alex had felt from Gill had worn off, replaced by something much more confusing. Gill's calm demeanor made him seem like an adult, so the occasional sparks of childishness were all the more apparent.

Gill was wearing his HUD visor, and he flipped it down when he knelt. "I've been tracking the trajectory of the meteor. A little while ago, I hacked into the Nest's server to look for their records on the meteor's path."

This was more than enough to get Alex's attention. "What did you find out?"

"The meteor was traveling faster than anything ever documented in the nine realms. When it entered our atmosphere, it came to a dead stop, and it hasn't moved since. This implies your hypothesis might be correct."

"I didn't know I had a hypothesis."

"There is more to the meteor than meets the eye. I hesitate to even call it a meteor. If it were a naturally occurring object, it would have smashed into the ground hours ago. Yet here it is, not moving at all."

Roy's voice crackled over Alex's comm. "Hey, kid, the floating eyeball is here. Head over."

Alex stood and brushed the dirt off her butt. "All right, that's my wakeup call," she said jokingly. "I'll see you guys in a bit. Hopefully, I'll know what's going on. Later."

Alex walked to where Roy had said the ship was going to be. She crested the hill, going in the opposite direction of the meteor. There she saw the ship. It was an elongated silver thing, looking almost like a cigar. Two huge thrusters were located on each side, and it carried numerous turrets. *Glad to see they came prepared for a fight,* Alex thought.

Roy, Toppinir, and a handful of soldiers were waiting at the ship's entrance for Alex. They nodded to acknowledge her and headed onto the ship. Alex followed, jogging to keep up with them so she wasn't walking behind anyone.

The ship looked as high tech as anything Alex had seen in the Nest. It appeared to be made of the same living crystal as the Nest as well. Soldiers and ensigns crowded it, giving the ship the feeling of a beehive.

The two veterans went straight to the holomap in the middle of the bridge. Manny was floating there, waiting for them. He smiled when he saw Alex. "Looks like you are incapable of following anything like an order or suggestion," he said and laughed.

Alex was glad the Beholder wasn't pissed at her. It seemed as if everyone in the room now took her much more seriously than they had a few hours ago. "Myrddin told me he recruited me to fight. I want to make sure I don't disappoint."

"You've scared the living hell out of all of us, but you haven't disappointed yet."

Roy looked like he didn't have time for pleasantries, his face grim and set. "All right, what do you have for us, Manny?" he interrupted.

Manny was all business as he looked at the holomap, which displayed the meteor above them. "Getting rid of the creatures surrounding the meteor was a great idea," he started. "Now you have a direct path to the hole Team Boundless created."

"And what good is a hole if we don't know what's inside it?"

"We've sent our best drones to try to get an idea of what we're up against. We haven't received anything back yet."

Alex listened to Toppinir and Roy discuss possibilities with Manny. Their concern revolved around not knowing what was within the meteor. That was when Alex had an idea. "Hey, Manny, can I borrow your eyes?" she asked.

Manny did a double-take as one of his tentacled eyes whipped around and stared at Alex. "What do you mean?"

Alex motioned for Manny to follow her as she headed toward the ship's exit. Once outside, Alex asked Manny again if she could borrow his eyes. This time the Beholder didn't bother replying. Alex closed her eyes and focused.

When Alex opened her eyes, she was seeing with Manny's abilities. She saw the heat signatures of everyone around her, along with their bones and a weird energy as well. Interesting but not what she cared about.

Alex looked up at the meteor and focused on zooming in while concentrating on Manny's x-ray vision.

As Alex stared up at the meteor, its outside edges blurred. She focused until finally, she saw into the interior of the meteor. The interior of the meteor was hollow, but other than that, Alex couldn't make out any more details. That seemed like enough, though.

Manny was growing irritated and bored. "You just wanted to take a look at the same thing we've all been looking at for the last few months?"

Alex headed back toward the bridge. "You can never have too many eyes, you know," she murmured.

When Alex got back to the bridge, she told Toppinir and Roy the meteor was hollow. She had been unable to see what was inside, but there was definitely room to move around.

Toppinir and Roy exchanged glances, then Toppinir said, "That's what we were thinking. Looks like our plan might work."

"What would that be?" Alex asked.

"We're going to infiltrate the meteor and blow it up from the inside, using a combination of Roy's nuclear reactor and my dragon's ether fire."

"Doesn't leave you guys with a lot of escape options."

"Nothing we aren't aware of."

The reality of what Toppinir was saying hit Alex. They were talking about sacrificing themselves to take out the meteor. Alex couldn't believe they would think of something so stupid. The war effort needed them. That was when another plan started forming in Alex's head.

Instead of speaking her mind, Alex asked, "What do you need from Boundless?"

Roy seemed taken aback by Alex's willingness to follow orders. "That's a new note for you."

"Well, we're here to help. No matter the cost."

"If that's the case, we'll devise a strategy and relay it to you to give to your team. Dismissed, Bound."

Alex nodded politely before heading to the ship's exit. She hit her comm button and patched into Jollies. "Hey, I need you to listen very carefully to what I'm going to tell you right now."

CHAPTER FIVE

Alex took her time rejoining her team. She relayed what Roy and Toppinir had said inside the ship. Both of them were ready to sacrifice themselves to take out the meteor, which seemed like a stupid idea. Two of the best fighters in the war, gone within seconds because they were supposed to be heroes.

What the hell was a hero, anyway? Who was asking them to do this? Was it just understood that they would sacrifice their lives for Middang3ard?

It was a waste, pure and simple, and it was exactly what Alex had come on this mission to try to avoid. Keeping track of what she was supposed to be doing had been hard since the mission had gotten so hectic, but now it was crystal clear.

The mission had been to save Roy and Toppinir. Two veterans blowing themselves up in a giant meteor would be nothing short of failure.

Alex hoped Jollies had paid close attention to the instructions she had been given. There wasn't a reason to doubt Jollies' competence. The pixie hadn't disappointed Alex or the team one time yet. The only reason Alex was worried was that she was asking her teammate to do something that could possibly end up badly for everyone.

Alex's comm dinged, and she pulled up her HUD to see what she had received. The briefing for Roy and Toppinir's mission had gone out. It included details for what everyone was expected to do and, in no uncertain terms, informed them of Roy's and Toppinir's decision.

There were no replies. This wasn't a discussion. The three squads were expected to arrive at the rendezvous and watch the fireworks. Alex wondered if Roy and Toppinir had really thought this plan through. There had to be another option.

Alex laughed to herself. If there had been another option, she might have thought of it, but she had drawn as much of a blank as the veterans had. It was a very extreme situation, and she guessed it warranted extreme measures.

The rest of the squads would be heading over to the rendezvous about now. Alex wasn't ready to go yet. She didn't think she was ever going to be ready.

Alex sat down on the grassy hill, leaned back, and looked up at the meteor. The thing was swelling, growing larger. She knew it. Yet it was also the same, unchanged. Whatever was in the meteor was responsible.

Even though it held signs of death, of destruction, the sky was rather beautiful. The red and black clouds had finally disappeared. In their place was a blue and blank sky with a thin green hue. The meteor stood in for the sun, covered in a hazy jade cloud.

For the first time in her life, Alex thought of taking a picture. She laughed at having such a mundane desire. She was standing on the precipice of the biggest decision of her short life, and all she could think of doing was taking a picture.

Alex slipped off her visor, turned it around, and snapped a photo of herself smiling, the meteor behind her. She looked at the photo. The tears in her eyes were visible. She wiped them away and took another one.

No tears this time.

Alex checked this photo. Good enough. She pulled the visor on again and hit the digital keyboard. A holographic keyboard appeared in front of her, and she typed a message to her parents. She would have preferred a video message, but she wasn't sure she could keep her voice calm.

I love you a lot. You'll never know how much because I'll never be able to tell you, not in the right words. But you have to know I do because you raised me to be the way I am. I can't thank you enough for being the kind of parents you are.

Tears were slowly streaming down Alex's face. She wiped them off and kept typing.

Something happened here. I don't know what being a hero is. I don't know what makes people do stupid things. So, if anyone ever asks, I wasn't trying to be a hero. I was trying to do something smart. I'm really sorry. Love, Alex.

Alex sent the message and dropped her visor, wiping away her tears and feeling stupid for crying like a child. Roy and Toppinir hadn't shed any tears. They had made their decision with straight faces, with determination.

Behind Alex, a twig snapped. Alex jumped to her feet. Gill stood behind her, his eyes glowing in the dark. "I see you're taking your time getting to the rendezvous," he said softly.

Alex wiped her face again, hoping Gill didn't see the tears or the snot. "Just wanted to take a little breather, that's all."

"We know what you're planning to do."

Alex couldn't meet Gill's eyes. Her lip quivered, and she wished she could crawl into a ball. Disappearing would be a close second. Everything felt too real at the moment.

Gill sat down next to Alex. They sat there quietly, watching the meteor above, expanding and contracting as if it were tearing open reality. Whatever was behind the meteor was beautiful. Alex didn't know what it was. She knew it was beautiful, though.

Gill rested his hand on Alex's and squeezed her fingers encouragingly. "I'm assuming there isn't anything we can say that'll change your mind?"

Alex shook her head as she fought back tears. Talking was making it worse.

"Jim is going with you," Gill told her.

Alex threw back her head, tears trickling down her face, staring up at the meteor—at her destiny. There was no point in fighting it anymore. She might as well accept what was happening. "He can't. He's not invited. I can't let him throw his life away."

"Surprisingly, that's what almost anyone would say to you. And it wasn't a question. Jim said he was going. None of us can stop him. Just like none of us can stop you."

"Did you come here to tell me that?" Alex asked.

"I assumed you needed someone to talk to. Jim couldn't come. He's too busy. Jollies can't believe this is happening. She's trying to talk Brath into tying you up or something. So, here I am. Figured you could use a friend right now."

Alex leaned her head on Gill's shoulder. "Appreciate it," she said softly, her voice cracking. "Gill, I'm scared. I'm really scared."

She didn't need to say it aloud. Her body was trembling, her skin like ice. The tears hadn't stopped, though they had slowed. Above, the meteor still watched like a menacing eye.

Gill put his arm around Alex's shoulder and kissed the top of her head. "Anyone would be. It's okay to be afraid. It doesn't make you weak. I couldn't do what you're doing. Never."

"What do drows think happens after you die?"

He chuckled softly. "It isn't a very encouraging belief we hold. You might want to talk to a pixie about that."

"Just tell me."

"Nothing. You just stop existing. That's why it's so important to enjoy life while you have it. To live as well as you can by your standards because you only have one life."

Alex leaned forward and wiped her face again. Sniffed loudly and spat. "You know, that's kinda encouraging. Gotta make the one count for something. Might as well get to it."

She stood and brushed the grass off herself. She felt the meteor watching her. It was unblinking. No need to blink since it could see everything. It could see deep within her.

There was a screeching sound somewhere far away. Alex could hear it, but she wasn't sure where it was coming from. It must have been close by, though.

When she woke up, blood was dripping from her nose. She was in the fetal position, her hands cupped around her ears, whispering words she didn't understand. Her chest was tight, and her head hurt the way it had when she'd first started using her eyes.

Gill knelt next to her, peering down at her, his bright eyes catching the little bit of light still in the evening sky. *This wouldn't be a bad last image before death*, she thought before becoming concerned about why she was on the ground. "What happened?" she asked.

The drow looked very concerned. "You tell me. You were standing, and suddenly you fell over. You spoke the Old Tongue. I couldn't understand what you were saying."

"The Old Tongue?"

"Old words of magic, magic that predates humans. I'm pretty sure those words weren't coming from you."

"Where from, then?"

Gill pointed up at the meteor. There was no denying it this time. The meteor was definitely larger than it had been when they had first arrived at the valley. "Whatever is in there," he said. "Maybe it's trying to talk to you."

"Why me?"

"You are the one planning on killing it, aren't you?"

Alex met up with the rest of Team Boundless, and they all headed to the rendezvous for the dragonriders and mechs. No one mentioned the plan, but it was palpable. It was the feeling of electricity, the scent of a grave, the cold chill of death.

They took their places amongst the other mech and dragonriders, waiting for Roy and Toppinir to arrive. If Alex was being honest with herself, the whole affair was a little gaudier than she would have imagined. It made sense, though. The vets had been with their squads for years. Leaving without saying goodbye would have been cruel.

The mech and dragonriders stood at attention, patiently waiting. They didn't speak amongst themselves. They watched the podium in front of the ship, where Manny floated in silence.

Manny looked uncomfortable. Maybe it was because he feared the riders would blame him for the loss of their commanders. How could they not? He was always the one bringing orders, showing up when things could only get worse.

A shadow hung over the gathering, cast by the meteor. The sky had changed even further. Gone was the green hue. Now images flashed behind the meteor, images which could not be understood, changing rapidly.

Jim described it to Alex as a television on the fritz or with bad reception. "There's something back there," he whispered. "That meteor's doing more than just sitting in the sky."

Alex understood what Jim was saying. "We're going to be the lucky ones who get to find out, right? You know what they say about curiosity."

"I prefer to think about the satisfaction part."

Alex grabbed Jim's hand. Even with all the confusion with Gill, this is what she had imagined ever since she had first seen Jim's avatar. "You know you don't have to do this," Alex whispered. "I'm not going to ask you to."

Jim curled his fingers around Alex's. "No one has asked me to do anything, just like no one asked you to do this. But like I said before, I'll follow you anywhere, Alex. Period."

"All right. Let's leave it at that."

Roy and Toppinir finally descended from the ship. They stood in front of the podium, looking out at the silent audience. Toppinir was the one to speak. "All right," he started, "I'm not going to drag this out. That meteor is coming down. Today. It's been a pleasure serving with you all."

Toppinir stepped back and Roy went forward. "Hm. It's gonna be hard to top that," Roy joked. "Toppinir and I aren't coming back from this, but you already knew that. I've seen a lot of crazy people in my day, but none as crazy as you. Every mission, you pull our asses out of the fire. This time it's our turn."

Roy raised his dragon anchor to the sky and his mech plummeted to earth, landing behind him. Its cockpit popped open as Toppinir's dragon uncurled from the top of the ship and crawled down. Toppinir mounted as Roy climbed into his mech.

Alex nudged Jim and whispered to Jollies, "Let's do this."

Jollies flew off as Jim left the crowd. Alex watched Jim walk away with a lump in her throat. She had no problem accepting responsibility for herself, but being responsible for Jim, her oldest friend, felt wrong. But it didn't matter. Alex raised her dragon anchor.

Chine came swooping out of the sky and grabbed Alex in his claws. He landed on the podium and shot a stream of fire into the sky in front of Roy and Toppinir as Alex climbed onto his back. "You guys can't go up there," Alex shouted.

Roy popped his head out of the mech. "Alex, this isn't up for discussion. You see what the meteor is doing, right? It's tearing up friggin' reality! We need to deal with it."

"Okay, sure, it needs to be dealt with, but it doesn't have to be you two. Myrddin needs you. *We* need you."

Toppinir shook his head, his eyes sad and heavy. "We aren't going to ask anyone to sacrifice their lives on a gamble," he explained. "We can't do that."

Alex slammed her hand to her chest. "You don't have to ask anyone. I'll do it."

Roy's face flashed red with anger as he ground his teeth. "We get it, you have a death wish," he lectured. "But we aren't going to entrust a mission this important to a cadet. It's not happening. Now, will you kindly get the hell out of our way."

Jim's mech climbed onto the stage next to Alex. "We're taking care of the meteor, sir. This is out of your hands."

As Jim and Alex argued with the two veterans, Jollies zipped around the stage faster than any eyes other than Alex's and Manny's could see. Yet Manny stayed quiet, watching from the sidelines as events unfolded in front of him.

Jollies flew back to Alex and whispered in her ear, "All right, you're good. Uh, I think you're a *great* person. I love you. I mean, as a friend. You know what I mean. Whatever. I love you, and I'm going to miss you." Jollies kissed Alex on the cheek and flew away, crying.

Alex fought back her tears. Now wasn't the time. She pulled up on Chine and they took to the sky, Jim right behind her.

Roy shouted, "What the hell are you doing? Get back

here!" He got back in his cockpit and powered up his mech. The machine surged forward for a second before whining loudly. It leaned to the side, struggling to stay up. "What the hell is going on?"

Toppinir pulled up on his dragon, but before it could take off, his dragon anchor started buzzing and sparking. The dragon anchor shut down, severing Toppinir's link to his dragon.

Jollies watched from the crowd, holding a bundle of cords and wires in her hand—the missing pieces from Toppinir's anchor and Roy's mech.

Above Jollies, Gill, and Brath, the two human riders, one dragon, the other mech, raced toward the meteor drifting in the sky.

CHAPTER SIX

The meteor had changed. There was no doubt now that Alex was closer. It had grown.

Substantially.

There was no longer a sky. The meteor seemed to have bled into it. There was no distinction between the two, only the green mist around the meteor.

Distance was an abstract concept at this point, as was time. Alex felt that for as long as she and Jim had been riding, they should have been closer. The extent of the meteor's influence was difficult to distinguish, but Alex knew it was responsible.

Whatever was inside the meteor was much more powerful than Holmorth had been, and extremely dangerous.

Alex felt like an insignificant speck compared to the sheer size of the meteor. It was nearly as big as an island. She couldn't see where it began or where it ended. Finding the spot where they had broken off a chunk earlier was impossible.

Jim's voice crackled over the comm. "That's not normal, is it?"

"Nope. That thing is definitely not normal."

Alex stopped flying. She just floated, watching the meteor above her. It was entrancing. She didn't know why, but she could keep looking at it forever.

Jim rested next to her. "How long have we been flying?"

Alex looked down at her dragon anchor. "Says here we've been flying for twelve hours," she murmured.

"No freaking way! We just took off. We did just take off, didn't we?"

Alex sat down on Chine's back and shrugged. "I have no idea. Nothing up here makes any sense. Like that," she said, pointing to the little bit of sky that could be seen behind the meteor, or perhaps the place where the meteor was most sky-like. "What the hell is that?"

A sharp pain pulsed through Alex's head, the same one that had brought her to the ground earlier. There was more pain this time, a hot flash, and then a sledgehammer cracking her skull open. Alex didn't fall down this time. She stayed conscious as her nose started to bleed.

It knew she was coming. Alex couldn't tell if whatever the meteor hid was scared or angry.

"You ever think you were going to die young?" Jim asked.

Up above, stars streaked by across the surface of the meteor, flaming balls of fire. "Not really," Alex answered. "I didn't really think about dying before. I guess it seemed like it was still pretty far away. My parents are pretty young, so it's not like it was on their mind or anything."

"My dad was afraid I was going to die young. You know, I don't think I ever told you this, but I almost died when I was a kid. Hospital ER and everything."

Alex glanced at Jim, who was poking his head out of his cockpit. He seemed so far away, as if his face were dragging miles and miles behind him. "No, we don't talk about a lot of personal stuff," she said. "What happened?"

Jim was quiet for a little bit, but when he started talking, Alex could hardly understand him. She didn't have to, though. Up above Jim's head, something like a movie was playing. She saw a small child waiting at a crosswalk. The child was reading a book, completely absorbed.

The child looked both ways, then stuck one foot out onto the street. Then the other. As the child crossed the street, a car came rocketing around the corner. It struck the child, and then everything was red. Everything was fractured.

Alex caught the last thing Jim said. "That's why everyone calls me Jaws," he explained. "Cause of the metal jaw I got."

"Did you talk to your parents? Before we left?"

Jim looked sad when he answered. "No, I didn't. And I didn't leave a message. I know my dad. It would mess him up pretty bad to hear it from me. My voice and stuff. It'd be better if the military told him. He could handle that."

Something like a projection of waves moving back and forth could be seen across the meteor. They were dancing with each other. Part of Alex wished the rest of the squad could see what she was seeing. It was beautiful.

The waves continued rolling, crashing against a large white wall. A cliff. There was someone standing atop the cliff. Alex. She was watching the waves. They were calling to her.

Alex watched as the waves parted. Her body lay on the ocean floor—broken, her eyes staring at her other self. Then the waves shifted and covered her corpse.

"We're still here, right?" Alex asked.

Jim was staring at the meteor. "I think so. It's hard to tell. This isn't anything like the last time we were up here," he answered. "This is...really freaky."

Chine's voice came through Alex's head, fuzzy and clear at the same time, like something crawling around in her skull. *It's a psychic projection. Whatever is inside the meteor is boosting the psychic connection of everything around it.*

Alex had no idea what any of that meant. *Could you say it in English, please?*

Our bond is psychic. The meteor is binding everything together. Somewhat. Not as strong as our bond, but there is a connection, and it's dripping into the air.

Do you think they can see it down below?

Definitely, but it looks different to them. Much like it looks different to each of us.

Is it an attack?

I'm not certain. It could be, but it's difficult to tell. Be on your guard.

Jim turned to Alex. His face was the only thing that made sense under the sway of the meteor above. At least Jim was constant. "I wouldn't have thought this would be the result of me playing a video game." He chuckled.

Alex giggled despite herself, despite where she was, despite the world falling apart around her. "Yeah, I wouldn't have guessed this would have come from that either," she admitted. "I'd probably get a refund if I could."

"You know, if I was ever going to do a heroic, hardcore, one-life playthrough, it would have been with you." Jim's face had gone serious, and he clenched and unclenched his fists. "You know, I kinda like you. A lot."

The lump in Alex's throat disappeared. "Yeah, I know. I like you too. A lot."

"Cool. Would it be corny if we kissed? Before we go off and blow ourselves up?"

"Let's wait until we blow ourselves up. Promise."

Alex stood, not wanting to ruin the moment but aware she had no choice. Up above, the meteor was changing. It was becoming something else while still increasing in size, spreading across the entire sky of Middang3ard.

A slit opened in the meteor, showing fold upon fold of what looked like flesh. The flesh quivered and gaped, dripping mucus as something with large, spindly legs forced its way through the fold's membrane.

Alex re-anchored herself to Chine, and the dragon started moving. "Come on. Looks like we're going to have to fight our way into the meteor."

Jim slid his cockpit shut and asked over the comm, "Why would I have assumed we wouldn't?"

Bats and bees burst from the mucous membrane of the meteor and swarmed around the opening, much like before. The only difference was there were thousands more of them. It reminded Alex of the last mission in *Middang3ard* VR. "Let's do this!" Alex shouted before taking off.

Jim was right behind Alex as they flew toward the swarming mass of monsters.

The monsters turned to the riders and attacked. Bats rushed them. Alex took evasive action, still trying to force her way to the meteor. There were too many bats, though. She was going to have to thin the flock.

Alex slammed her fist to her chest, unleashing her dragon anchor's power. Her body and Chine's burst into flames as they swerved to the outside of the swarm of creatures hellbent on their destruction. Chine let loose a funnel of ether fire, scorching through a handful of bats.

A bee came in high, swooping down and trying to take off Alex's head with its stinger. Alex pulled out her scythe and sliced through the bee, splitting its body in two.

Jim was having his own problems. He was unable to move as fast as Alex, but he had a huge amount of firepower. He fired a volley of missiles as he doubled back, getting himself into a better position and locking on to as many targets as he could. Conserving his missiles was a must.

The sky filled with the sound of Jim's guns as he mowed through as many bees and bats as he could.

Alex swung over to where Jim had made his stand. Chine activated his gravity well, causing the creatures closest to Alex to bunch together as if they were magnetized. Then the dragon kicked the cluster of creatures toward the meteor.

Once Alex was positioned beside Jim, Chine unleashed another torrent of ether fire at the swarm of bees and bats heading for him. The scent of scorched flesh filled the air. "We're doing it," Jim shouted. "We're cutting through them!"

It was too soon for Alex to celebrate. She was busy watching the flesh in the center of the meteor. It was quivering again, which meant something else was coming. She knew that whatever it was, it was going to make the bats and bees look like nothing.

First, two alabaster legs shot out as if something was being birthed. The legs were long and insectoid, and two more quickly followed. Then a head, sharp and elongated, burst through. The thing roared, showing rows of sharp teeth.

The creature's back was arched as if it had once had wings. Its bones protruded from its back, giving the impression its spine was going to burst free—and then it did. The creature's back tore open. Two beautiful, angelic, feathered wings sprang from the wound.

The creature flapped its wings as it screamed its bloodlust, then took to the sky. It was followed by another creature, and then another.

Within seconds, the meteor's fold was ripped open as thousands of the winged angels came pouring out of the rock's gash.

Jim sighed loudly over the comm. "Guess, I spoke too soon."

Now wasn't the time for despair. The moment their hope faltered, this was over. She needed Jim to stay with her. That was the only way they were going to get into the heart of the meteor. "We got this, Jaws," Alex shouted. "Those things can die just like anything else."

And Alex proved it. She leaned forward, sending the dragon rocketing toward the angels, spewing fire as she swung her scythe and hacked through anything in her way. The bees and bats fell as she neared the angels.

Most of the angels were still congregated on the meteor. Gravity wasn't working the usual way on it. The angels clung to the surface, walking upside down, hissing at Alex's approach.

Alex hit the side of the meteor hard, unleashing a blast of ether fire as her anchor's power wore off. She leaped off Chine and charged for the closest angel. The creature reared up on its hind legs and slashed at Alex, who dodged out of the way and cut it open.

Behind Alex, the dragon was burning through as many angels as he could while the bees and bats swarmed around them, trying to cut off access to the meteor's opening. "Come on, Jaws," Alex shouted. "We're getting in there!"

Jim hit his thrusters and plowed through the bees and bats in front of him, shooting anything that made the mistake of being in his way. Dozens of bats and bees fell to the ground as Jim forced his way through the wall of bodies.

It only took a few minutes for Jim to land next to Alex. He killed his thrusters and hit his leg stabilization, sinking his mech's feet into the surface with a heavy whirring of gears. Then he popped out of his cockpit and winked at Alex. "I'm with you, Captain. To the end," he said.

The angels were still swarming out of the meteor's opening. There was no sign they would stop anytime soon.

This was where Alex was making her stand. They weren't far from the opening. All they had to do was keep moving forward. As long as they were moving, they were alive.

Chine was right behind Alex, shooting fireballs as Alex took a step, slicing through an angel in her way. Another angel leaped at Alex. The dragon grabbed the angel, slamming it into the ground.

Six angels leaped onto Chine, sinking their teeth into his scales. The dragon roared as he rolled over, trying to crush the angels under his weight.

Alex saw Chine in pain and ran to his side, sliding across the meteor, hacking through the legs of the angels in her way as she went. She was so close. Then she felt a cold hand clutch the back of her neck, and she was flying through the air before she realized it.

The wind went out of Alex when she hit the meteor. Her vision went blurry for a moment before she was able to pick herself up. She grabbed her scythe and took in the scene before her.

They were being overrun. Angels were pouring over Chine like ants over a dead body. The same with Jim, who was firing every gun he had, his head poking out of the cockpit, his face slathered in blood and viscera.

This was it. This was Alex's last stand.

Two jets of fire scorched the meteor, burning through the angels attacking Chine and Jim. Alex looked up to see where they had come from.

Brath, Gill, and Jollies were racing toward her, firing everything they had at the angels, bats, and bees overwhelming Jim and Alex. "You thought we were going to let you have all the fun?" Brath shouted as Furi unleashed another torrent of fire.

The rest of Team Boundless burned through the angels

blocking the meteor's opening. There was just enough space for Alex and Jim to storm the meteor.

There was so much Alex wanted to say to the rest of the team. There wasn't time for it, though. Instead, she smiled and saluted them. Then she climbed back onto Chine and took off, Jim following closely behind.

CHAPTER SEVEN

Once Alex and Jim passed into the meteor, everything changed. The temperature rose drastically. Neither of them could hear anything from outside the meteor, despite being only a few feet from the opening.

If Alex'd had more time, she would have stepped in and out of the meteor to see if this was all in her mind, but that didn't matter right now. Hopefully, the meteor wouldn't exist for very long anyway.

As Alex and Jim flew through the interior tunnel, Alex weighed their likelihood of success. The plan had been Roy's and Toppinir's. She had no idea what their odds of success had been. They must have been fairly high, though. Both men had been willing to bet their lives on it.

But what if something went wrong? The meteor had grown since Roy and Toppinir had initially planned to blow it up. Or was it an illusion?

Alex didn't know what was real anymore. What she had seen outside as she and Jim were closing in on the meteor had left a lot of questions. Chine had said it was some kind of psychic projection. That meant it wasn't real, right?

None of those questions were bringing Alex or Jim any closer to what they were looking for—the core of the meteor. There was something powering the object, and they needed to find where it was and destroy it.

Alex pulled up her HUD visor and peered through it. She was looking for a source of energy, anything giving off a power or heat signal. There was nothing. As far as she could tell, the meteor was all one temperature.

The only thing Alex had to go on was the brief glimpse she'd had of the interior when she was looking through Manny's eyes. For the first time in a while, Alex wished Manny had come along for the ride. He would have hated this, though.

A pang of regret stabbed Alex in the chest. She pushed it down. Thinking about how much she was going to miss that floating mass of eyeballs wasn't going to help anyone. Still, it hurt to think about it.

Alex and Jim flew out of the tunnel into a vast, empty space. It was difficult to imagine this place was in the meteor, considering how large it was.

The walls were lined with holes. It would be easy enough for Chine and Jim's mech to fit through them. The problem was that Alex had no idea where they went. Each tunnel was a shot in the dark.

Jim poked his head out of his cockpit before climbing out of his mech and sitting on top of it. "You know what's really weird?" he asked. "I haven't seen one monster since we got here. Do you think the meteor sent all its forces out when we attacked it?"

Alex shook her head. That seemed too good to be true, but the other option was terrifying. If all those angels hadn't been the majority of the meteor's forces, how many could be hiding and waiting for them?

Jim shrugged before getting back into his mech. "Either

way, we should probably be careful. Getting ambushed in this creepy-ass place sounds horrifying. So, which one do you want to start with?"

Alex looked around the room, trying to figure out which tunnel to choose. "You know, maybe they weren't expecting us to get in," she mused. "That was a pretty crazy fight out there, and it's not like there's any surveillance equipment around. Maybe we're a surprise."

"I'd be surprised if the magical meteor floating in the sky and distorting reality had to rely on cameras to know we were present."

"Good point. We should get moving in case there are more of these creepy things in here. How about that one?" Alex asked, pointing to the largest tunnel near the ground.

"Works for me."

Jim and Alex descended into the room. When they landed, both of them gasped.

The floor was covered in a mix of eggs and plants. The plants had bulbous purple sacs with a stem reaching up to the ceiling. They were roughly three feet tall and gave off a disgustingly sweet smell.

There were thousands of them clustered tightly together.

Alex flipped up her HUD visor and took a picture of the floor, which she sent to Roy and Toppinir. "Whatever the hell these things are, it's not good. Even if we blow this thing up, I'd like to know Roy and Toppinir will destroy them if any manage to escape the explosion."

Jim had exited his cockpit again and was staring intently at the egg sacs. "Yeah, these things give me a really bad feeling." He shuddered. "We should get going. I don't want to be here when those things crack open."

They made their way to the tunnel she had pointed out and flew through it. While they were passing through, Alex aimed a light at the wall.

The walls of the tunnel were covered in writing etched deep into the rock. Alex recorded a little bit of the writing and sent it to Gill. "This place keeps getting weirder and weirder," she muttered to herself. "You ever see anything like this, Jim?"

Jim's voice crackled a little over the comm. "Yeah, I have," he answered. "They're runes, Nordic or something. I used to play a game that had a lot of Norse mythology. Some of the puzzles used runes as a device. I don't know what they mean, though. I've never seen most of them."

Norse runes? In a meteorite filled with evil monsters that was above Middang3ard? Yeah, things could definitely get stranger.

Alex hardly knew anything about Norse mythology. She'd studied the bare minimum of Norse history for her home-schooling classes. All she knew was that there were warrior gods, and the Vikings were always invading someplace.

Maybe that's all this was. The meteor was just a ship for an invasion. Wouldn't that be something?

The tunnel Alex and Jim were taking split into three different paths. The two of them banked right and continued on, heading farther into the maze of tunnels. They began to feel lost. Alex wondered if they were getting any closer to the center or if they were just flying in circles.

Jim pinged Alex and she hit her comm. "Hey, you know that energy scan you did a while ago? I just did another one, and I'm starting to pick up some energy discharges. You should run another one and let me know what you get."

"Gotcha."

Alex swiped up her visor and ran the scan again. Jim was right. There was an energy discharge coming from some-where in the tunnel. She locked onto it and said, "All right, now we have something to work with."

The two of them sped toward the signature. It wasn't easy

since the tunnels they were in didn't always lead in the right direction. There was a lot of backtracking and doubt, but Alex knew they were getting closer because her head was hurting more. Whatever had caused her headaches before was in here.

Chine squeezed through a new tunnel, wiggling to make it larger for himself. *I don't have a good feeling about this*

Alex directed her thoughts to the dragon. *What do you mean? We're on a suicide mission. What would you feel good about?*

The energy we are moving toward is powerful. More powerful than I thought. Much more.

So what? Doesn't mean it won't blow up. We'll be cool, Chine. And by cool, I mean we're going to blow this thing sky-high. Trust me.

I do trust you, Dustling. You have great courage.

Alex realized she hadn't talked to the dragon about what she had decided to do. When the meteor blew, it wasn't just going to take Jim and Alex. He was going to be caught in the blast as well. *Oh, my God, Chine, I didn't even ask you about all this. I am so sorry.*

There is nothing to apologize for, Dustling. Where you go, I go. We are bound to each other. Our lives will always be intertwined.

I still don't understand the whole binding thing. Have you got a minute to explain it to me?

It is a binding of fates. Mortals don't understand life outside of themselves, even the long-lived ones such as dragons and elves. There is always fate. It is unseen and unheard, but it can be touched. In our case, our fates have been bound together until our death.

Alex laughed as Chine took a hard left. *You know, that's almost romantic*

Chine did not laugh. *No, it is not. You do not want to know the extent of bonding that dragons find romantic.*

Maybe I don't. Let's just leave it at that.

They flew in silence for some time before Alex spoke again. *Are you cool with this? I mean, you're not an old dragon.*

And you are not an old human. To answer your question, yes. Yes, I am okay with this. The Dark One's forces must be stopped. I am happy to help in any way I can. There is purpose in that. Solace, even.

Alex checked her visor for the power signature. They were very close. "Hey, Jim, I think the power source is coming up in a little bit," she called. "Maybe to the left this time...I hope."

Jim answered, "I'm glad you are taking care of directions. I have absolutely no idea where we are, but left it is."

Alex and Jim turned left and exited the tunnel into an open space much like the room full of eggs they had seen when they entered the meteor. "Ugh, I hope this isn't another gross room," Alex groaned. "I'd like to die without being covered in goop."

Jim's mech pointed at the ceiling. "Alex, look!"

Alex followed Jim's finger and looked up.

The ceiling was covered in what could only be called veins. They were massive things, as big around as a bus, pumping and quivering. They were crisscrossed like a spider's web, hanging from the rock of the meteor.

In the middle of the ceiling was a thing like an eye but not made of flesh. It hung from a bundle of veins like a piece of rotting fruit. The energy was coming from that.

Alex and Jim landed at the bottom of the room. Thankfully, there were no eggs. "What the hell is that?" Alex asked as she stared at the ceiling.

Jim exited his mech, staring up at the red mucus-covered eye hanging over them. "I have no idea, but that's the energy source. Whatever it is, it's in control of this whole place."

"You see those things all over the ceiling? They look like feelers or tendrils. Or like earthworms."

"I don't care what they look like. I just want to know if this is the place we're supposed to be blowing up."

Alex jumped off of Chine and paced around. "You know, maybe this whole 'sacrificing ourselves for the good of existence' thing doesn't have to happen," she said, thinking aloud.

Jim asked, "Are you seriously thinking about backing out now?"

"Hardly. I'm just thinking, we didn't know there was this much energy coming off that thing when we got here. Maybe we can just pull the plug on it. And if we can't do that, we could set off your mech. Start a chain reaction and get out of here before it blows."

Jim thought about the plan Alex had just proposed. "You know, that's not a bad idea," he finally assented. "And I'm pretty stoked about the part where we don't die."

"Yeah, that's kind of my favorite part of the whole thing, too," Alex agreed. "If we make it out alive, I'm gonna want more than a peck from you. Full-on Twilight, all right?"

Jim blushed brightly but didn't turn away. "I can definitely promise you some Twilight-level sparks," he boasted.

"Great. Let's do this."

Alex climbed atop Chine and anchored herself. *Let's go, buddy.*

Chine didn't move. The dragon stayed rooted to where he was, staring at the eye above them. *I can't. I can't move.*

What do you mean, you can't move?

The eye or whatever it is is keeping me from moving. The headaches we've been having, the psychic projection outside the meteor—it's all telepathy, coming from above.

Alex couldn't believe what she was hearing. *Are you telling me that thing is alive?*

It is alive and aware of me. I do not think it has recognized you or Jim yet.

Alex wracked her brain, trying to figure out what options she had. If Chine couldn't move, she couldn't get close enough to the eye to do any damage. Then a gamble popped into Alex's head. *Hey, Chine, did you mean what you said about me becoming a strong psychic?*

Chine groaned as he tried to move. *I do not see why that is important at the moment, but yes. You have a tremendous amount of raw talent.*

How about we find out right now? Can you boost my whatever the hell it is strong enough that I can connect with that thing? Maybe I can force it to release you, or at least take a look at what we all look like from up there.

Alex, I think that is a very bad—

We don't have a whole lot of options right now. Can you help me or not?

Chine was quiet for a moment. Finally, he said, *Yes. I can. But I will not be able to help you past that.*

Great. That was just icing on the cake. *Wouldn't have it any other way, my dude. Patch me in.*

CHAPTER EIGHT

Alex did not close or open her eyes. She did not know when the change came, but it had been sudden, and she was no longer in the same place in time. Wherever she was now was a place outside of all that. She was aware of very little. Her body? Her mind? Perhaps they were here. She did not know.

All around, nothing but darkness beyond anything Alex had ever experienced. Darker than blindness, darker than the years spent alone, fumbling through books with her fingers. Darker than the quiet dreams that brought her screaming into the waking world.

Alex tried to feel around, tried to grasp where she was, tried to make sense of what she was experiencing. It did not last long. Each moment she spent trying to understand what she was experiencing made it more difficult to grasp.

In the darkness, there was a light. It was not bright, nor was it dark, yet it was all-consuming. Alex saw it, and she did not see it. In any other situation, the paradox would have driven her wild. Now, it was merely the current state of affairs.

Alex had heard many times in life that you were never supposed to go toward the light. Obviously, she would. Curiosity never faded. In or out of her body, Alex needed to know.

The light was humming. It was the hum of something lifeless, of machines working without any knowledge, of a bug zapper waiting for its next kill.

Alex went to the light. She could not tell if she was running, but she was moving as fast as she could. It wouldn't be long now.

Blinding—that was the only word Alex could think of, and she understood the irony. She stood before the light, watching it, waiting to see what was going to happen.

Somewhere out in the dark, someone was speaking. Alex couldn't hear what they were saying, nor did she care. It was just noise. The light was interesting. There was something special about the light. That was why Alex was here, fighting her way through the darkness. It had something to do with the light.

Then it was gone. There had been no warning. The light simply disappeared. Then the darkness disappeared as well.

A young boy stood before Alex. The child only came up to Alex's waist. She had no idea how old the child was because there was a mask over his face. The mask was made of wood—a deer with swooping horns, the face painted with white chalk.

The boy's black eyes peered from behind the mask. "What are you doing here?"

Alex felt like she should kneel to be on the same level as the child, but she remembered what Brath had told her about insulting gnomes. "I'm not sure," Alex admitted. "What are you doing here?"

The masked boy pointed into the darkness. "I'm traveling," he said. "There's a place I'm going. It's been a long time since I've seen anyone. What's your name?"

"Alex. Alex Bound. What about you?"

If the boy heard her question, he gave no sign of it.

Seeing he wouldn't answer her question, at least not now, she asked, "What are you waiting for?"

"I'll remember when I see it."

The darkness grew bright with runes, shining as if they were stars—the same rune, over and over as far as the darkness extended. Alex wished she knew what the rune stood for. Its repetition brought no insight into its meaning.

The masked boy started to walk. It did not seem as if he thought he would be followed, but Alex walked after the boy. "Is there anyone else here?" Alex asked.

The boy stopped. It was not as if he stopped walking, but rather that his body no longer had any weight. It was as if he shimmered in and out of existence, waiting to be called back, yet unwilling to wait for the calling. "Yes, there's someone else," the boy answered.

"Can you take me to him?" Alex asked.

"Sure. He's cruel, though. I'm not sure you would like him."

The two walked through the darkness, the light flickering around them like the darkness was filled with thousands of pixies. "Do you like him?" Alex asked. "Do you want to hang out with him?"

The boy stopped walking, looking around as if there were answers to be divined in the darkness, in this place where there was nothing but everything at once. "No, I don't," the boy said. "I don't like him at all. But I'm stuck with him. Bound to him."

Alex thought of Chine and their intertwined destinies before answering, "Yeah, I know what you mean. At least, I think I do."

The two continued walking, pilgrims of the night, unaware of that which they strode toward, yet heading toward it nonetheless.

Alex could not tell when her legs started to hurt, nor when she realized she had legs. Slowly, memories came flooding back to her. None of this was real. This was a psychic projection—Chine had told her that—but she wasn't outside anymore, so It couldn't be a projection. She was inside something.

The masked boy stopped walking and pointed to the light. "Go in there," the boy said. "That's where he is. The one you want to talk to."

Alex, against her better judgment, knelt and looked the boy in the eye. She reached out and touched his mask. The boy didn't protest. Alex pulled the mask off.

The unmasked child did not have black eyes. One was the brightest, clearest blue Alex had ever seen. The other was a black hole as dark as death. The boy's face was covered in soft freckles, and his hair was sandy blonde. Even though he couldn't have been any older than ten, his eyes held the age of the ancients. "What's your name?" Alex asked.

The boy was silent, his lip quivering as if he were uncertain of being able to speak such a profane thing. "Forni," the boy finally said. "That is what everyone calls me."

"It was nice to meet you, Forni."

"You too."

With that, the boy was gone. Alex stood alone before the light. Her heart was racing. With Forni gone, Alex remembered why she was in the darkness and what she was doing. She was looking for a way to save Middang3ard, and that way seemed to be in the light.

Alex took a deep breath and stepped inside.

A shriek tore through Alex's head, heard and unheard.

She thought it had just been in her head until she opened her eyes. Then she saw the truth.

The light was emanating from a black hole, a large tear in reality. Planets, stars, and time were swirling around it. Alex felt drawn to the black hole, but she refused to move.

That was when the eye focused on Alex. It came from the black hole, but she did not know how. She could not see the eye, but she could feel it watching her, peering into her, piercing her skin, crawling through her chest. The eye saw every single thing.

Alex did not know when she began screaming, but she feared she would never stop.

Before her was an eye, nothing more and nothing less. It floated in the blackness, its veins massive and terrible, quivering and shaking as it rolled its iris toward Alex, slow and awful as the tide of a tsunami.

The eye trembled, and the darkness swelled and screeched as Alex stood before it, wishing she could run and knowing there was nowhere she could flee. *How are you here?* came a voice, crashing through Alex's head.

The sheer power of it reduced Alex to tears. She did not know when she fell, but she embraced the darkness beneath her, screaming to cover the reverberating words echoing in her brain.

HOW ARE YOU HERE?

Alex felt her mind unraveling. It was not a slow process. There was sanity, and there was insanity. She almost slipped from one to the other.

No, she thought to herself. *You are here for a reason. The mission. Remember the mission.*

Alex forced herself to stand. Her nose was pouring blood and her head was pounding, but she made it to her feet. "Who gives a crap?" Alex managed. "I'm here. What the hell are you doing here?"

A wave of psychic energy blew past her. It was like having her head ripped open, dissected, and displayed. She tried to hold it together, but it was impossible. Her thoughts lay splayed out for the eye to see.

The eye swelled as its veins grew redder. *How dare you?* the voice thundered.

Alex felt another wave of energy coming at her. She imagined herself far away, standing atop a castle, looking down at a horde of warriors rushing toward her. The walls would hold. She knew that. "You're the Dark One, aren't you?"

There was no answer. The eye continued to twitch and swell. Alex had expected an answer. This gave her an idea. "You are, aren't you?" she asked again. "I would have expected the Big Bad to be more intimidating. I didn't know we were fighting a giant eyeball."

The darkness expanded and then contracted, becoming tangible. Alex felt it creeping across her skin. It didn't matter, though. She didn't understand what was going on, but she knew how she was going to play this out. It was a battle of minds, of wills.

The Dark One's voice lashed out as the eye constricted and then grew larger. *How dare you speak to me? Do not dare to question me. You are nothing but a speck. I will crush you.*

"Yeah, yeah, okay, I got you, but why are you just an eye? Is that, like, all you got?"

Alex felt her body pull away from her. She had no idea where it went, but she was floating separate from all physicality. She saw the meteor, and she was the meteor, all of its tunnels and corridors stretching out before her as if they were her body.

Another screech ripped through Alex's mind. The sound was nearly enough to send Alex into the darkness, but she remembered why she was here. She guarded herself, not fully realizing what she was doing, but it worked. The darkness peeled away, showing her the Dark One's eye.

"What the hell are you?"

The answers came at her faster than she was able to process. There was a meteor, which she could see. A thousand bodies fell into each other, biting and tearing at each other's flesh. A scream, speaking a language she had never heard.

Alex was on her knees, trembling as the eye quivered. She tried to pull herself together. *They're just thoughts. That's all,* she thought. *That's all.*

Then the true nature of the Dark One's eye was revealed.

CHAPTER NINE

The Dark One's eye filled the entirety of the liminal space. Alex was aware that she was both inside and outside of the Dark One. Was this what she always experienced when she looked through someone's eyes? Was there this much connection?

A force pushed Alex down, and she went skidding across what felt like water. She was drenched when she finally came to a stop. The eye was now the sun beaming down on her

When the Dark One spoke, it radiated through Alex. *You are a waste, all of you. A waste of potential. Humanity. Elves. Dwarves. You could all be so much more. I will show you how. Through me, you will know perfection.*

Alex watched as a meteor, the same meteor she was currently inside, passed through the sky. The meteor fell to the earth, crashing into the ground, tearing through anything in its path. As the meteor impacted the earth, millions of tendrils slipped out of the rock, latching onto the ground, forcing their way under the soil.

Alex was inside the meteor. Or inside the meteor inside

the Dark One's head within the meteor. It was confusing. She thought it better not to think too much about it. But from inside the meteor, she could see where the tendrils were coming from.

The meteor was hollow. The tunnels Alex and Jim had flown through were paper-thin. That must have been how the meteor had been able to store so many monsters. And now the monsters were gone, the tunnels filled with throbbing red tendrils.

Alex followed the tendrils down the tunnels until she came to their source. She stood before the Dark One, his veins pulsating as his eye quivered. "That's your big plan?" Alex asked. "You're the thing Myrddin is so afraid of? A giant parasite?"

The Dark One's laughter bounced around in Alex's head, the sound of a thousand screeching voices. *No,* the Dark One said. *I am not even a fraction of what Myrddin fears. This form is merely a vessel for my will. It is nothing more than an old skin cell to me.*

"And what are you planning on doing with this old skin cell?"

Expanding. Righting and uplifting. I will become Middang-g3ard, and the realm will finally be elevated to perfection. The realm will be like me.

Alex giggled and tried to stifle the sound. She thought it might be rude. Then the sheer ludicrousness of The Dark One's idea made her burst out laughing, holding her sides as the eye watched. "Are you kidding me?" Alex asked, still bubbling with laughter. "That's your evil scheme? Your manifesto is that you want everyone to be like you?"

When the Dark One spoke, Alex heard something she hadn't heard from him before. It sounded almost like doubt. *I wish for all in existence to be perfected,* the Dark One repeated.

"And your idea of perfection is to be exactly like you? I'm

assuming you think you're perfect. You have to, even though you're a floating eyeball. I mean, realistically, even your dead skin cells should be a shining example of what existence could be. I'm kinda underwhelmed."

Alex felt herself becoming larger. Maybe it was physical or just in her head, but whatever she had said was making her more powerful. "You think you're some kind of god, don't you?" Alex asked. "You really think you're divine?"

The Dark One's voice thundered loudly. *Do not waste your words, human. You are already beaten. I will crush Middang3ard beneath me and remake it in my image. You have already lost.*

"Oh, my God, you can't take criticism either. Now you're going to get all loud and pouty with me because your origin story sucks. Not gonna lie, I'd have to rank you pretty low on the villain spectrum. I'll give you props for style, though. The whole psychedelic meteor thing was pretty cool."

The Dark One was vibrating with rage but silent. Alex took a seat, waiting for the Dark One to speak. When the silence began to bore her, Alex said, "You know we haven't lost. Not even close."

I will be within Middang3ard's soil by the end of the night. My power will extend all through the realm, and I will suck it dry until it bends to my will. Then I will reshape it as I please. Every living creature will bear my image within them.

"Yeah, yeah, I gotcha. You're spending a whole lot of time explaining your master plan to a kid because you're scared."

The Dark One said nothing, but the color of the sky changed to a deep crimson. Alex was now floating in a boat. There were no stars in the sky, no clouds. The masked boy sat across from Alex in the rowboat, his knees pulled tight to his chest.

The eye of the Dark One hung heavy in the sky. "Hey," Alex said to the child. "That thing up there scare you?"

The child looked up at the Dark One's eye. "Yeah, it does. I don't like it. Not at all."

"So, I'm thinking about making that thing go away. How would you feel about that?"

The boy pulled up his mask, his blue eye peering deep into Alex's soul, his dead eye glowing the same hue as the Dark One's eye above. "I'd like it to go away," the boy said.

"What happens to you if the mean guy up there goes away?"

The masked boy pulled his mask back down and looked over the side of the boat. "When he goes, I go too. But maybe it's better that way."

Rage, pure unfiltered and destructive, radiated from the Dark One's eye. He knew what Alex was doing, and he was not pleased.

Alex wasn't sure what she was doing, but by now, she knew enough to trust her gut. She didn't need to know what the boy was in relation to the giant eye in the sky, but she could piece together enough to know the boy with the missing eye was somehow related to the Dark One's eye.

Alex rose, rocking the boat slightly. "All right, kid, it was nice to meet you. I'm going to put a stop to this. Uh, thanks for talking."

The masked boy leaned over the edge, drawing his hand through the water. "You are right," the boy said. "He *is* afraid. That's why he's so angry. He wasn't lying, though. This is only a piece of him. There're many pieces of him. Of me, I guess. Even when you destroy this version of him, there are more."

"That's all right. Just means I gotta kill them all."

Alex closed her eyes, focused on finding Chine. The world around her melted away and she heard Chine's heart beating. *Hey, I'm ready to get the hell out of here. This place is way too weird. You mind helping me?*

Chine's voice echoed as if he were speaking in an acoustic chamber. *Concentrate on your body, Dustling. Bring your mind back to it,* he explained.

Oddly enough, Alex didn't know how to imagine her body at first. She still hadn't gotten used to seeing her reflection in the mirror. Even if she tried, she couldn't really think of what she looked like—except her hands. Alex knew her hands better than her features.

She imagined her fingers running over a page of braille, the stammer of the bumps, the edges of the paper as she turned the page.

When Alex opened her eyes, she was lying next to Chine, his wing over her. Jim was sitting at her side, holding her hand. He helped Alex sit up as she rubbed her eyes. "How long?" she asked.

She stumbled to her feet with Jim's assistance. "Way too long," Jim answered. "I thought you were dead, but whatever you did in there worked."

Jim and Alex stepped out from under the dragon's wing. The eye hanging from the ceiling had changed dramatically. It was still large, but now it looked as if it had been pumped dry of all its fluids. The veins around the eye looked weaker.

Alex anchored herself to Chine as Jim stepped back into his mech. "All right, let's go ahead and wrap this up. This whole place is hollow like a wasp's nest, and you know how easy it is to break one of those up. All we need to do is set off your mech, and we're good to go."

Alex and Jim took off, flying toward the eye. Alex was glad to put all of this behind her. She could finally go back to the Nest and deal with all the trouble she was going to be in. At the moment, death sounded much easier to handle.

The two riders hovered below the eye as Jim primed his mech for detonation. Once the mech was ready, he climbed into Chine's extended claw. The dragon tossed Jim onto his back, and Alex anchored Jim's feet to the dragon. "Cool. Let's blow this thing," she said.

Suddenly, Alex felt her body go stiff. It was as if someone had stepped into it. She tried as hard as she could, but she didn't budge.

Jim noticed Alex's frozen face. "Everything okay?" he asked.

Before Alex could try to answer, she felt an intense pain in the front of her brain. That pain quickly spread until her entire body was wracked with it. The meteor broke apart around her and she was falling, her mind on fire. A thousand voices jabbered in her head. She didn't know which was hers. Then a voice louder than any of the others shrieked loud enough to shatter her skull.

The voice took a form that far exceeded what Alex was capable of understanding. Looking upon the form filled her with mindless dread and the desire to run away screaming, to hide and hope she was never found.

"I fear nothing!" the Dark One boomed.

She knew then she was not going to die. What she was going to experience would be a thousand times worse, her mind rotting before her, flailing in the burning presence of the Dark One's essence. It was already happening. She could feel herself drifting.

Chine's voice rang in her head amongst the chorus and cacophonous screeching. *Dustling! It is not your time yet. Do not give up!*

Alex held onto her dragon's voice. She tried to use it to support herself, to drown out the voices behind her, the screaming and raging hatred so pure it threatened to submerge her entire existence.

Suddenly, she was back in her body. She slumped and Jim grabbed her, keeping her from falling off Chine. "Do it now," she whispered before contacting Chine and saying, *This one is all you, buddy.*

With the last bit of her energy, Alex reached out to the Dark One. She imagined her hand wrapping around its hanging eye, and she focused all of her ideas and intent into the image. Then she saw herself ripping the eye from the ceiling.

An audible scream filled the cavern. Jim took that as his cue and detonated the mech. The mech's reactor melted down as Chine flew away. They had only thirty seconds before the mech exploded. It wasn't nearly enough time.

Below, angels crawled out of the tunnels. They stared up at the eye as if curious.

Chine raced away from the Dark One's gaze while Alex held on as hard as she could. She struggled to stay conscious as the dragon swerved through the tunnels, Jim shouting directions as he gripped Chine's neck to keep from flying off.

The angels were crying, a loud wailing throughout the meteor. Then there was an explosion. They heard it even though it sounded far away. The walls of the tunnel shook violently, rock falling from the ceiling. "We're almost out of here!" Jim screamed. "Just hold on."

Holding on was all Alex could do.

Chine shot his ether fire and broke through the side of the meteor as the flames from the explosion followed on his tail, shooting out as if the meteor was a flaming dragon.

The flames hit the dragon and he spiraled out of control. Alex reached out for Jim and pulled him close, holding him as tight as she could while Chine fought to right himself.

Another explosion cracked the meteor down the middle, sending rock and debris flying. A chunk of rock hit Chine on his wing as fire scorched the dragon's tail.

As the meteor blew to smithereens, Chine fell from the

sky. To the dragonriders on the ground, it looked like a meteor shower, Chine burning as bright as the brightest shooting star.

CHAPTER TEN

Alex woke up in a bed in a white room in the Wasp's Nest. The crystal walls projected a calming, muted white light. When she tried to move, her head felt dreamy and distant. The world quickly came into focus as she attempted to pull off her sheets.

Nothing happened. Alex looked down. Her right arm was missing from the elbow down. There were no bandages, only a nub.

A sick feeling started in the pit of her stomach and raced up her throat. She held her right arm close to her chest as she cried. The sickness left with the tears, and the tears gave way to a realization: she was still alive.

She pulled the covers up to her neck with her other hand and sat very still. She listened to herself breathing. Tried to move the fingers that were no longer there. Let the silence of the room and the crystal glow of the walls pass over her. She drifted back into sleep.

There were no dreams, only a blank kind of rest. It was just what Alex needed.

When she woke up again, Myrddin was standing next to her bed. "Good morning, Alex," he said.

She sat up, careful to keep her bedsheets covering her right arm. "Hey," she said groggily. "I'm assuming we won."

"All because of you. That stunt you pulled was foolhardy, rebellious, and dangerous. And thanks to you, Middang3ard is safe for some time. I cannot thank you enough."

Myrddin waved his hand, and a chair flew from the other side of the room to him. He took a seat and sighed heavily. "I'm sorry for your loss. You had a multitude of visitors trying to storm your door, but I thought it better for you to have some time to yourself in light of what happened."

Alex removed the sheet and looked down at where her arm had been. "Kinda funny, right? You give a blind kid her sight, and then she goes and cripples herself. That's ironic."

"Actually, that is poetic justice."

Alex groaned as she leaned back. "Are you seriously going to quiz me on literary terms right now? Your bedside manner is atrocious."

"Wizards are not known for indirectness. Which brings me to my second reason for being here. We will be having many talks in the future. Chine has informed me of your psychic potential, which is something we will want to develop. But before that, we must talk about your arm."

"What's there to talk about?"

"An armless rider is a liability. You have two choices: a magic arm or a cybernetic arm. Both are ready to be attached whenever you are ready, should you wish to remain as a dragonrider."

The matter-of-fact way Myrddin spoke about Alex's injury put her at ease. This was just part of the job. Riding wasn't the same as it was in VR. There were real consequences; Alex understood that now. "I'll take the cybernetic arm," Alex said after thinking for a while. "Actually, it sounds pretty cool."

Myrddin stood and magicked away his chair. "That was what Jim believed you would say. Would you prefer to allow your visitors in before or after the operation?"

"Before. As soon as possible."

"They've been waiting outside for you to wake up."

Alex smiled as she stood up. *Still got two legs*, she thought. *Could have been worse.*

Myrddin headed to the door. "Hold on," Alex called. "What about Chine? Is he okay?"

"Why don't you ask him yourself?"

Alex turned her thoughts to the dragon as Myrddin politely waited by the door. *Chine, are you okay? Please tell me you're okay.*

Chine answered instantly, his voice much more excited than usual. *Alive and well, Alex. Fire is the least of our worries for dragons. How are you? Myrddin told me the extent of your injuries.*

Well, I get a robot arm, which I think is pretty damn sick. Glad to hear you made it out all right.

Glad to have you finally awake. I was beginning to worry.

Alex turned to Myrddin, flashed him a smile and a thumbs-up. He opened the door and let in the other riders. All of Team Boundless waited at the door, as well as Roy and Toppinir. Before Alex could say a word, Jollies rushed into the room and wrapped her arms around Alex's neck, sobbing loudly.

Alex had to peel Jollies off like a band-aid. "I was so worried about you!" the pixie cried.

Alex sat Jollies in the palm of her hand and said, "If I had been conscious, I would have been worried about you too," before looking around the room and saying, "I'm glad you all made it."

Out of the riders, Jim and Brath were the only ones who

looked banged up. The side of Brath's neck had been burned badly, but it seemed to have mostly healed, no doubt through magic. Jim had a scar running across the side of his face, and he was in a cast.

Alex had grown used to being stared at, but the intensity everyone looked at her with was unnerving. "Uh, so, how much trouble am I in?" she asked.

Toppinir rested his hand on Alex's bed. "None," he said. "The level of bravery you showed was beyond anything the dragonriders have seen. The meteor was destroyed because of you. Middang3ard owes you and Jim a deep debt."

Roy fidgeted awkwardly at the back of the group before he pushed his way forward. "What was inside the meteor?" he blurted. "What did you see? We tried to get Jim to tell us, but he said he wasn't sure what he was looking at. What about you?"

Alex held the nub of her right arm as the riders tried not to stare. "It was the Dark One," she whispered. "Or at least part of him. There was a child too. I think it might have been him, or an older version of him. It was all kinda confusing, but I know for a fact that thing was the Dark One."

"You talked to him, didn't you? What did he say?"

"He talked a lot about wanting to take over Middang3ard, about reforming it in his image. The guy sounds like he has *really* deep ego issues, but I think that probably goes without saying."

Alex took a deep breath as she tried to put the last few hours into words. "Honestly, it was terrifying," she admitted. "I don't really know what that guy is, but he's insane. And scary as hell."

Myrddin interrupted the solemn silence in the room. "That we already knew. No need to think about it for too long. For now, we will celebrate. A decisive blow has been struck to the Dark One."

There was a murmur of agreement before Myrddin started to shoo the visitors from the room. Before Myrddin could force Gill out, he got close to Alex and whispered in her ear, "Glad you made it." Myrddin got the drow by the collar and tossed him out.

Jim was the only one who managed to avoid Myrddin's paternal hurricane. He sat down on Alex's bed. "Didn't think I was going to get a minute with you before the whole ceremony."

"Jaws, don't be weird. You know you can have as much of my time as you want."

An awkward silence filled the air as Alex wondered what she was supposed to say. Should she just wait for Jim to do something? There should have been a manual. "Hey," she eventually said. "Come over here."

Jim skootched over to Alex. Alex grabbed him by the shirt, pulled him down to her face, and kissed him. It was a gamble, but it paid off. Jim slipped his hand around Alex's neck, returning the kiss.

When they pulled apart, Jim's face was flushed, and he tried to catch his breath.

Alex's heart was racing in her chest, and she giggled nervously. "We should do that a lot more."

———

Alex sat in front of her room's window, watching the new cadets flying their dragons for the first time. She looked down at her new arm. It was still in its skeletal phase, so the gears and wiring of the cybernetic arm were visible. Even so, the arm was an elegant piece of machinery.

She flexed her fingers, then closed them to make a fist. She was glad Myrddin hadn't wasted any time getting her the new arm. The best part was, the arm felt as natural as though it had always been a part of her body.

There was a knock on the door. "Come in," Alex said.

Myrddin and Jim stepped into the room. The wizard wore a fashionable pale-blue suit. Jim was wearing his dragonrider uniform, the same one Alex wore. "Getting to be about that time?" she asked.

The wizard nodded, opening the door wider. Alex rose from her bed, cast one more glance at the cadets in the field, and exited the room.

The mess hall of the Nest had been transformed into a banquet hall of such elegance, foreign dignitaries could have been hosted within it. She saw table after table covered in delicious concoctions, reflecting the various races enrolled in the dragonrider program.

The mech riders were amongst the invited guests. Most of their tables boasted human delicacies. They were, in fact, a mostly human riding corps.

Team Boundless sat in a place of honor near the stage. There was a general murmur throughout the hall. Everyone was waiting for Alex to give a speech.

Alex stood behind a curtain on the stage, trying to calm herself. She had never spoken in public before, and she had nothing prepared. Myrddin had only told her she was expected to give a speech a few minutes ago.

Not knowing what else to do, Alex reached out to her dragon. *Chine, what am I supposed to say?*

Chine did not answer immediately, but Alex could tell he was mulling things over. *Mortal creatures are very sentimental. You should speak from the heart. Do not overthink it. Just be yourself. That is who they are here to listen to.*

All right. Guess I'll see how that works out. If I bomb, I'm blaming this on you.

Alex could hear Myrddin talking past the red curtain. "And now I introduce to you the first human dragonrider," Myrddin called.

That was Alex's cue. She took a deep breath and walked out.

The lights were very bright, and at first, Alex couldn't make out anyone in front of her. Slowly, everything started to come into focus. She could see Team Boundless sitting near the podium and the rest of the dragonriders filling the room.

Alex tried not to think about what she was going to say as she hobbled across the stage. She was still pretty beat up. The audience patiently waited for her to get to the podium, and she cleared her throat before taking a deep breath.

When Alex spoke, her voice was shaky, almost cracking. "So, we won the battle, I think," she joked. The crowd chuckled politely as Alex summoned her courage and went on. "You know, I saw what the Dark One was in the meteor. Part of that was terrifying, but the rest? The rest was pathetic. I saw what he's planning on doing. He thinks he can improve us. He thinks we are weak, and we'll be stronger through him. What do you guys think?"

A chorus of voices shouted their disagreement, slammed their hands on the tables, and clinked their glasses. "Exactly," Alex shouted back to the crowd. "This war is far from over, but I'm damned if I spend it running from the Dark One."

Alex raised her cybernetic arm and clenched her fist. "We will fight. We will bleed. We will sacrifice." She let her words hang over the crowd for a moment before speaking again. "We're taking this fight to the Dark One. I am a dragonrider. The *first* human rider, sure, but I promise you this: I will not be the last. Dragonriders, the Dark One is coming back, but we are ready," she said as she looked at the cadets, at Toppinir, at Roy, at Brath, Gill, Jollies, and Jim, and with unbridled pride cried out, "And we will win!"

The shouting and war cries of the dragonriders could be heard long into the night. They were accompanied by the roaring of their dragons.

The sound would have frightened anyone.

Even the Dark One.

The End

Alex and Jim are on a date in Middang3ard. Sadly, Middang-g3ard isn't very romance-friendly … and when a comet pursued by the Dark One's forces crash lands onto the surface, Jim and Alex have to cut the date short to investigate in *Love and Aliens*.

AUTHOR NOTES RAMY VANCE
FEBRUARY 13, 2020

Since we're so close the April Fools (at the time of publication), I had to share what I did last year. Check it out!

Hey everyone! Check out my new series:

Tired of the same old urban fantasy plot lines? Looking for something brand new and mind-bending?

Check out Ramy Vance's new series: The Toddler...

The Toddler is coming. Pray he hasn't missed his nap.

Prone to tantrums, resistant to sleep and perpetually hungry, this pint-size hero has just soiled himself.

It seems that a powerful magic has befallen the city, putting all the adults to sleep. And now there's no one around him to change his dirty diaper.

Now The Toddler must risk all to save the adults from their endless slumber.

But time is running out, for if he doesn't find a cure soon, he's going to have one hell of a diaper rash.

If you like the Dresden Files, Mercy Thompson or Buffy

the Vampire Slayer, then you'll be helplessly addicted to The Toddler series.

COMING SOON!

Praise for The Toddler:

★★★★★ "Finally a breath of … well … seriously stinky air."

★★★★★ "Buffy meets Dora the Explorer."

★★★★★ "Move over Paw Patrol … Adventure Bay finally has a real hero."

There are three more covers, but because of space issues, I couldn't put them here. I have them on my Facebook feed and/or join my Facebook Group: House of the GoneGod Damned ... all the covers, plus this year's April Fools are in there!

THANK YOU for reading our story! We have a few of these planned, but we don't know if we should continue writing and publishing without your input. Options include leaving a review, reaching out on Facebook to let us know, and smoke signals.

Frankly, smoke signals might get misconstrued as low hanging clouds so you might want to nix that idea.

I live on the strip in Las Vegas and it is presently one week since I got back from London and five days since most of the hotel-casino's on the strip shut down due to the efforts to contain Covid-19.

I live next to the Aria, beside the Cosmopolitan, and across the street (and a block or two down) from the MGM Grand and New York New York casinos.

The Aria and New York New York are important because the restaurants I frequent are inside them. You know, inside where I can't even get take-out anymore.

Presently, it is 1:30PM in the afternoon and traffic on Las Vegas Blvd (always a mess on Friday nights and Saturday afternoons) *is not a mess.*

In fact, the whole strip is about 95% shut down. There are a few restaurants open including Giordano's (we are helping them stay open and paying a few workers), McDonald's, a hot dog place in front of Bally's (I can't remember the name but purchase a Mexican Coke every time I am over there) and also Wahlburgers. Plus, any CVS or Walgreens (which seem to occur every few blocks near my place.)

I have a theory why we have any traffic at all.

Theory: People from outside the strip (think Henderson or RedRock area) are taking a drive to see the strip closed. The expectations of no cars traveling up and down is doomed to disappointment because of sightseers coming in to see the absence of cars—therefore, there are cars.

Well, it's only a theory.

This morning, I went up and down the strip buying a little from each of the stores and trying to give everyone a little business. Of course, I cleaned hands wherever I went as I walked through the stores looking for a bit of TP or anything we might be able to use that didn't require refrigeration.

I purchased frozen dinners from a Walgreens across the street because the manager personally showed me the Walgreens app and the items in the freezer on sale. I explained I was walking back and couldn't carry that much.

She told me to take the little shopping cart on wheels and simply return it.

I bought more than I technically needed at that store and I WILL go back. Not only to return the cart (it's so damned cute!) but also to support them and their efforts to stay open when the strip is closed for business.

I wish I had a larger freezer to help them more.

However, I hit two CVS' and two Walgreens' plus a Target and I scored one roll of tissue paper. That's not a package of 4, 12, 16, 24…it was *one* from all five stores.

They had about thirty single rolls on the shelf, so I took my one and felt like I had downed a 14-point buck at 200 yards through trees so thick it looked like a fence.

(Is fourteen points a good-sized deer rack? I really don't know as I don't hunt. If you were nodding your head with my story, remember I am *paid* to lie for a living. It's a good life.)

If you live here in Las Vegas, remember that the little (*expensive*) stores on the strip have way fewer shoppers. One of our people inside LMBPN mentioned that no one remembers that truck stops often have toilet paper. I tried that.

They didn't .

I suppose it is possible there is a different side of the store than the one I went into to find the elusive TP. Where I looked, it was a seriously small shelf space that was empty. *Hmmm.*

I should have called Stephen Russell (Author S.R. Russell) who was a truck driver for a few decades to ask him before I left there empty handed the other day. Well, not truly empty handed as they had buy-1-get-1-free on M&M's. I figured why the hell not? We might need protein (peanuts), emotional healing (chocolate), and calories (sugar) in order to survive the next few weeks.

There, if you needed an excuse to buy Peanut M&M's, you're welcome. If you don't, I applaud your lack of concern when purchasing junk food. I had to give myself a reason to load up on them.

I've used that damned 'sugar is calories' excuse a LOT in the last 7 days.

Take, for example, the following 'food' I purchased using the sugar is calories excuse.

It has *Mike* in the name. How can I not support *THAT???*

For now, we here in the Cave in the Sky™ are doing fine. Neither the wife nor I have tried to suffocate each other yet, nor have we tried to toss each other out of the windows. Fortunately, I purchased a mattress topper a month ago to put on my couch in the office for naps. If I need to, I can hang out here if the wife starts to moan....

BRAIINNNZZZZ.

All joking aside, this is a new time in our world. The challenges we have encountered will be overcome, the new society that comes out the other side will be interesting. It's time for those who can to help those who need it.

For those who need help, raise a hand when your neighbors ask.

I am grateful to you our readers who read our books. Later this week, we will place a few of our books (all of them) for children out for free, paying the young author for the privilege. We are not a children's publisher, so we do not have many selections. Look for Sienna Lawson.

OTHER BOOKS BY THE AUTHORS

Other Middang3ard Books

Never Split The Party (01)
Late To the Party (02)
It's My Party (03)
Blue Hell And Alien Fire (04)

Death Of An Author: A Middang3ard Novella

Other Books by Ramy Vance

Mortality Bites Series
Keep Evolving Series
Fatebound Series
Welcome to the Dragon Show Series

Other Books by Michael Anderle

For a complete list of books by Michael Anderle, please visit:

www.lmbpn.com/ma-books/

All LMBPN Audiobooks are Available at Audible.com and iTunes. To see all LMBPN audiobooks, including those written by Michael Anderle please visit:

www.lmbpn.com/audible

CONNECT WITH THE AUTHORS

Connect with Ramy

Join Ramy's Newsletter

Join Ramy's FB Group: House of the GoneGod Damned!

Connect with Michael Anderle and sign up for his email list here:

Website: http://lmbpn.com

Email List: http://lmbpn.com/email/

Facebook:
www.facebook.com/TheKurtherianGambitBooks